•• THE CARVER CHRONICLES ••

DOG DAYS

BY Karen English

ILLUSTRATED BY Laura Freeman

Houghton Mifflin Harcourt

Boston · New York

For my grandson, Gavin —K.E.
For my mom —L.F.

Text copyright © 2013 by Karen English
Illustrations copyright © 2013 by Laura Freeman

All rights reserved. Originally published in hardcover in the United States by Clarion Books, an imprint of Houghton Mifflin Harcourt Publishing Company, 2013.

For information about permission to reproduce selections from this book, write to trade.permissions@hmhco.com or to Permissions, Houghton Mifflin Harcourt Publishing Company, 3 Park Avenue, 19th Floor, New York, New York 10016.

www.hmhco.com

The text of this book was set in Napoleone Slab.
The illustrations were executed digitally.

The Library of Congress has cataloged the hardcover edition as follows:
English, Karen.
Dog days / by Karen English ; illustrations by Laura Freeman.
pages cm.— (The Carver chronicles ; book 1)
Summary: Gavin wants to make a good impression at Carver Elementary, where no one knows he excels at soccer and skateboarding, but an annoying big sister, a bully, and his great-aunt's Pomeranian are not helping.
[1. Moving, Household—Fiction. 2. Schools—Fiction. 3. Friendship—Fiction.
4. Great aunts—Fiction. 5. Bullies—Fiction. 6. Pomeranian dog—Fiction.
7. Dogs—Fiction.]
I. Freeman, Laura, illustrator. II. Title.
PZ7.E7232Dog 2013
[E]—dc23
2013001826
ISBN: 978-0-547-97044-8 hardcover
ISBN: 978-0-544-33912-5 paperback

Printed in the United States of America
16 2021
4500824613

• Contents •

One
It Was an Accident!

Gavin is waiting for his new friend, Richard, to come over to play video games. Gavin likes Richard, his friend at Carver Elementary. Gavin had lots of friends at his old school, Bella Vista Elementary, but he knows that you have to start over whenever you change schools.

In this new neighborhood, there's a lot to get used to. There's the new house and the new backyard and the new kids on his street who don't even know that he is practically a soccer star. Well, maybe not a *star*, to be exact, but he thinks he's pretty good. Anyway, Richard chose him for his team in kickball, so Richard's a nice guy.

Gavin has his socks rolled into a ball, and while he waits, he tosses the sock ball up hard until it hits the ceiling and comes back right into his hands.

"That's annoying. Why don't you stop?"

It's Danielle, his sister. Unfortunately, she was not left behind at the old house.

He tosses the balled socks up at the ceiling again just to spite her.

"Ugh. You're so annoying!"

Luckily, she's going across the street to babysit. *Soon,* Gavin hopes.

Finally, the doorbell rings — and before he can get up to answer it, Danielle, Miss Big-Eighth-Grader, Miss Big-Thirteen-Trying-to-Be-Sixteen, opens the front door and stares down at Richard.

"Yeah?" she says, in her new cool manner.

Richard stares up at her for a few seconds. "Are you Gavin's sister?"

Without answering, Danielle calls over her shoulder, "Gavmeister, your friend's here."

Gavin cringes. No one knows about that nickname at his new school. Danielle steps aside and lets Richard in. He tiptoes past her, probably a little afraid of her looming presence.

"Hi," he says sheepishly from the living room doorway.

"Hi," Gavin says. He throws his balled socks at the

ceiling once more and catches them easily, hoping Richard's impressed.

"Are we still going to play video games?" For some reason Richard seems a bit unsure.

"Yeah. What do you want to play?"

Richard shrugs and plops down on the sofa. "You have *Fight Night*?"

Gavin stops tossing his sock ball and sits on the floor, staring at the blank screen of the television. He hates to admit that his mom doesn't allow "overly violent" video games. "No, I don't have that one."

"You have *Slam!*?"

Gavin shakes his head.

"*Slam 2!*?"

Gavin shakes his head again.

"Well, what *do* you have?" Richard asks, frowning.

"I have *Animal Incredible.*"

Richard looks at Gavin as if he's grown a third eye. "Man, that's a baby game."

Gavin doesn't say anything.

Richard sighs. "Okay, we'll play that."

After twenty minutes Gavin can tell, without even looking at him, that Richard is getting tired of the game. He's sighing and making mistakes and Gavin knows it's just a matter of time before the complaints begin. They're both sitting on the floor now with controls in their hands, trying to rack up points to add particular animals to their kingdoms. Gavin is racking up more points than Richard, so he isn't surprised when Richard puts the control down and says, "This game sucks."

Gavin looks over his shoulder quickly. His mother doesn't like that word. "It has a rude sound," she'd explained the one time Gavin tried it out. "I don't want to hear that again."

"That's 'cause I'm winning," Gavin says to Richard.

"Because you play this baby game all the time." Richard gives the control beside him a shove, to show that he is totally finished with trying to populate his kingdom. "Who cares, anyway? Why don't you at least have *Spooky Mansion*? Carlos has it, and it's way more fun."

"My mom likes games to be kind of educational," Gavin admits.

Richard sighs extra loud. A big sigh that begins with a long intake of breath. "Whatcha got to eat?"

Before Gavin can answer, he hears his mom on the stairs. She stops in the room with her purse over her shoulder. "Hi, Richard," she says.

Richard looks like he's suddenly on guard. "Hi, Mrs. Morris."

"I've got to go to the mall," she tells them. "Your dad's in his office, and Danielle is right across the street at the Myerses'. You guys going to be okay?"

Gavin stifles a smile. It's always a relief when his sister is out of the house. If she isn't pinching him for no reason when she walks by, she's pointing out that his ears are too big for his head. He *knows* his ears are too big for his head. But everyone has a little something that can be improved upon. Danielle is sprouting tiny pimples on her forehead, signaling more to come. (He can't wait.) That Deja girl in his class is probably going to need braces, and Richard's nose is kind of big and funny-looking.

"We'll be okay," Gavin says. He doesn't ask what there is to eat, because then his mom will tell him all the things he'd better not get into. Like the cookies or the chips or the fruit bars she usually lets him have for an after-dinner treat.

As soon as the door closes behind her, he smiles broadly, feeling the glow of freedom. Even though his dad is two rooms away, it's almost like he has the house all to himself. He looks over at Richard, who's now tossing the sock ball up to the ceiling. "Want some of Danielle's candy?"

"Yeah. Where is it?"

"In her room. Under her bed." Gavin grins mischievously. "She doesn't know that I know where she keeps it."

They both start up the stairs, and the closer they get to Danielle's candy, the more thrilled Gavin gets.

"She's gonna know we took some," Richard says.

"No, I've done it before. You just rearrange the pieces in this tin thing they come in. Kind of spread them out to take up the empty space. You just can't take too much. I do it all the time." He walks through Danielle's room to the window and checks the Myerses' house across the street. All's clear.

Richard is still cowering in the doorway as if he's afraid to enter the room.

"Come on. What are you afraid of?" Gavin asks.

"She could come back any minute, and she doesn't look very friendly."

"I can tell you now, Danielle is definitely not friendly."

Richard steps into the room but stays near the door. He looks around at the bed with the pink canopy, the pink throw rug, and her collection of tiny ceramic animals on a shelf above the dresser. Three photos depicting ballet dancers are framed in pink.

"Lotta pink in here," Richard says.

"If you had a sister, you'd know they love pink."

Richard picks up a tiny ceramic giraffe and squints at it.

"Put that down — and I mean right where you found it!" Gavin cries.

Richard places it back on the shelf. Gavin moves to the shelf and squints at the giraffe. "Is that *exactly* the way it was?" he asks.

"I — I — I guess," Richard stammers.

"'Cause if it isn't, she'll know I've been in her room! Look at it closely, Richard."

Gavin dashes to the window and checks the house across the street again. All's still quiet. No Danielle stomping back home. "Come on, let's hurry," he says over his shoulder. He drops to the floor beside Danielle's bed, reaches way underneath, and pulls out the tin of candy.

"Why does she keep it under her bed?" Richard whispers as if there is someone to hear him.

"To hide it from me." Gavin laughs his cackle laugh. "*Haa, haa, haa.*" He's been practicing. He's gotten it to sound almost like Mr. Muddlemouth on the *Captain Radical* cartoon. Laughing makes him feel less nervous.

Richard looks over at him and smiles with appreciation.

The pink tin of candy has a snug top that's kind of hard to pry off when you're in a big hurry. Gavin tugs and tugs at it. He can feel his heart beating. Suddenly, he stops and listens. "What was that?"

"What?" Richard asks.

"Shhh," Gavin says. Was that the Myerses' front door? Is Danielle already on her way back home? Gavin jumps up and dashes to the window once more. Across the street, nothing is happening at the Myerses' house. No Danielle. He looks over at Richard, who's peering at Danielle's animal collection.

"No more touching Danielle's things, Richard." Gavin picks up the tin and gets the top off. The gold-foil-covered chocolate nougats inside always look like treasure to him. He picks two, then carefully spreads out what's left to fill the empty spaces. He replaces the lid and pushes it back in its place under Danielle's bed. Then, just as he stands up, before he can turn toward Richard, he hears, "Hey, catch!"

Richard is sailing Danielle's snow globe — the one she got the previous winter when her middle-school choir traveled to New York City for a festival, the one made of heavy glass and not plastic — right at Gavin. But unfortunately, Gavin is a half second too late getting his hands up, and the heavy glass globe hits the corner of Danielle's dresser and shatters. Water and suds and the tiny Empire State Building and shards of glass fly everywhere.

Gavin and Richard stand there for a full five seconds silently staring at the mess that was once Danielle's precious snow globe, her prized souvenir from New York City. Gavin scoots to the window again to look across the street at the Myerses' house. They have to work quickly. "First we have to get the glass up!" he says to Richard, who seems to be stuck in place. Gavin dashes to his room and gets his trash can. Carefully, he begins to pick up the biggest pieces of glass first.

"You should have caught it," says Richard. "I said, 'Catch.' Why didn't you catch?"

Gavin is being super careful as he deposits the larger pieces of glass into his trash can. Next he needs to vacuum up the tiny pieces.

Gavin hurries to the bathroom to get a towel to sop up the water. He throws it at Richard. "Get the water up so I can vacuum!" He runs to the hall closet for the vacuum cleaner.

Within minutes, the tiny plastic Empire State Building and the big pieces of glass and the plastic base are in Gavin's trash can hidden under some wadded-up paper towels and the rest of the glass is inside the vacuum cleaner. The only telltale sign that something has happened is the slightly darkened spot on Danielle's bedroom rug next to the dresser.

Richard breathes a big sigh of relief. Gavin steps out of the room, then quickly steps back into the room to see what can be noticed at first glance. How fast do his eyes go to the wet spot? he wonders. They go to it pretty fast. Maybe because he already knows it's there?

They tiptoe down the stairs. He doesn't know why they're tiptoeing. They go out the front door and sit down on the top porch step to wait — for whatever's going to happen.

"Maybe I better go home," Richard says.

"No," Gavin insists. "You're in this with me. Just wait. As

soon as my mom gets back, I'll ask if we can go to the park. Then we can be gone when Danielle gets home."

Ignoring that, Richard says, "What will your sister do" — he swallows — "if she finds out we went into her room?"

"You mean what will she do if she finds out we went into her room, stole her candy, and broke her snow globe from her one-time trip to New York?"

"Yeah," Richard agrees in a small voice, after a moment.

"You don't even want to know," Gavin says. Then it's his turn to swallow with fear.

● ● ●

The Myerses' front door opens then, and Danielle steps out.

"Shoot, shoot, shoot," Gavin mutters. Apparently Mrs. Myers came back from her supermarket trip sooner than he expected. She stands in the doorway with Luna, her two-year-old, on her hip. She waves Luna's hand at Danielle. Danielle calls out, *"Adieu, ma chérie! Bisous!"* The two-year-old waves back. Danielle's taking French this year, and Gavin has to hear this kind of stuff all the time. Her French is driving him crazy.

Danielle skips across the street and stops in front of

Gavin and Richard. She looks down at them with a tiny smirk. "What are you two up to?"

"Nothing," Gavin says, looking past her. "We're just sitting here."

She frowns and then squints. "I'm picking up a funny vibe. What's going on?" She looks at Richard. Richard looks down.

Danielle makes a sound of blowing air through her lips. She steps past them, and Gavin hears the door close. He holds his breath to see if he can hear her running up the stairs to her room. Gavin looks over at Richard. "Where was the snow globe before you threw it at me?"

"It was on her nightstand," Richard says.

Gavin's heart sinks. "Shoot. She's going to know it's gone right off."

They both sit very quietly, listening.

As if on cue, Danielle's voice starts low, then builds up like an ambulance siren. "I don't *believe* it! I don't BE-LIEVE it!"

Why does Gavin's mother have to pull into the driveway just then? Before she can even get out of the car, the boys hear Danielle coming down the stairs. It sounds as if she's taking them two at a time. She comes barreling out the front door, then leaps off the porch to stand right in front of Richard and Gavin with her hands on her hips.

"I don't BELIEVE it!"

"Believe what?" Gavin asks. He keeps swallowing as he widens his eyes to look as innocent as possible.

"Yes, believe what?" Gavin's mom says. She's gotten out of the car and is coming up the walkway toward the three of them, a shopping bag in her hand.

It's as if Danielle has not even heard their mother. She doesn't take her eyes off Gavin. "WHERE'S MY SNOW GLOBE?"

Gavin's mouth falls open with dread. "It was an accident," he finally manages to say.

"What happened? And you'd better tell me the truth!"

"Danielle, please keep it down," their mother says.

Gavin stays silent and looks to his mother for help.

"He's always messing with my stuff, Mom! I tell him to stay out of my room, and he goes in it anyway." She turns her angry, pinched face back to Gavin. "What were you doing in my room, Bozo? Did you take this clown into my room too?" She tosses her head toward Richard, and Richard leans back. Gavin sees him gulp.

"No name-calling, Danielle," their mother says calmly. "Let's go in the house." She turns to Richard. "Richard, I think it's time for you to go home."

Danielle immediately protests. "He needs to explain himself first. I know he had something to do with it, and he needs to stay here and explain himself!"

Gavin looks over at Richard again. He's lost all his toughness. He looks petrified.

"Let's get this straightened out in the house." Something in their mother's voice tells them she isn't going to say it again. She sighs. "Come on in, Richard."

Once inside, they all stand in the entry hall while Gavin's mom taps gently on his dad's office door. Gavin's dad steps out and looks from one to the other. "What do we have here?"

Danielle elbows Gavin hard and scrunches her face at him. "Tell him, Gavmeister!"

"Let's go in the dining room," Gavin's mother says. She leads the way. When they've all taken a seat, Gavin's dad says, "I can't wait to hear this."

Danielle doesn't wait for Gavin to explain. "Dad, I'm all the time telling this guy to stay out of my room. And he totally disrespects my space and —"

Gavin's dad turns to Richard. "How do you figure into this?"

"Me?" Richard's eyes widen. He turns to Gavin.

Gavin looks down and mumbles, "I told Richard that Danielle keeps some candy under her bed. And I asked him if he wanted a piece. He said, 'Yeah,' so we went in there just to get one piece each, and —"

"Did you ask Danielle?" Gavin's father asks.

"I couldn't, because Danielle was across the street." Gavin looks to Richard, and Richard nods his head.

"So you thought it was okay to just go in there and take some candy anyway."

Danielle glances from Gavin to Richard and gives them a smile that seems more like a sneer.

"I'm really disappointed in you, Gavin. First, you set out to do something wrong, and then you involved your company."

Richard looks down as if he's an innocent victim of Gavin's as well.

"But, Dad . . . it wasn't like that. Anyway, Richard was

the one who messed with Danielle's snow globe. He's the one who threw it at me."

Richard pipes up with, "But I said, 'Catch,' and you should have caught it. Then it wouldn't have broken."

"I think we've heard enough, Gavin," his mother says. She turns to Richard. "Richard, you may go home now."

"And I didn't even throw it hard," Richard adds as he gets up and starts for the door, looking very relieved. He doesn't even glance back as he leaves.

"See, Mom? And Dad? See how he's always disrespecting my space? I think he needs to be put on punishment. It's only fair."

Gavin looks down at his hands, waiting for the verdict. He listens to the front door close. Now he's on his own.

"I'm going to think about this," his mother says.

"There will be a punishment," his father says. "You can count on that."

Danielle raises her chin in triumph. She smiles at Gavin. One of her snarly smiles.

"You can be sure we'll come up with something," his father adds. "Something appropriate."

"Right now I have things to do," Gavin's mom continues. "Your great-aunt Myrtle and uncle Vestor are coming over for dinner tomorrow."

Oh, no, Gavin thinks. It can't get any worse than Aunt Myrtle and Uncle Vestor coming to dinner. He has a feeling his troubles are just beginning.

Two
Eat Those Peas!

Uncle Vestor and Aunt Myrtle come to Sunday dinner once a month. Aunt Myrtle is really Gavin's dad's aunt, so she's Gavin's great-aunt. But everyone just calls her Aunt Myrtle. It's no fun when they come to visit, because Gavin has to become a completely different person. He has to say "Yes, ma'am," "No, ma'am," "Yes, sir," and "No, sir." He has to remember to eat with extra-good table manners.

Throughout dinner, he has to listen to Aunt Myrtle's long list of complaints and put up with the sharp looks that she gives him when checking to see if he's eating with extra-good table manners. And when Uncle Vestor drops the usual quarter in his hand, which isn't even enough to buy a candy bar, he has to look really excited and say, "Thank you, Uncle Vestor." At least they've left Carlotta at home today.

Carlotta is Aunt Myrtle's Pomeranian. She's a horrible

dog with a fierce little wolf face, strange orange fur, and a way of making this low, growly sound from the back of her throat. She doesn't like Gavin, and Gavin doesn't like her. She's too nervous — she yaps all the time and runs around Gavin's ankles, threatening to nip at them. He doesn't know why she acts that way around him. Maybe he gives off a funny scent.

Now Aunt Myrtle is complaining about a pain in her hip. Uncle Vestor is silently chewing his mashed potatoes, looking as if he's heard this complaint five million times. Aunt Myrtle thinks she might have to have hip-replacement surgery like her friend Gert. She goes on to explain how the surgery didn't work and how Gert is still having hip problems and that it would be just her luck to still have the same difficulties too.

Then she goes on to talk about her heartburn troubles and how she has to sit up in bed all night just to get to sleep. And then, of course, there's talk of Carlotta. Gavin thinks of that little yapping mouth and how Carlotta's small head jerks a bit with each bark. He imagines sharp nibbling at his ankles. It almost makes him put his chicken leg down.

"I don't know what I'm going to do when Vestor goes on his trip next week to the Barbershop Harmonizers'

Convention. When he comes home for lunch, he always walks her." Uncle Vestor not only owns a barbershop on Marin Street, but he's also part of a singing group made up of real barbers. They sing for weddings and parties and stuff. Gavin has seen their act a bunch of times. He thinks about the Crooners now. That's what they're called: the Barbershop Crooners.

Just then Gavin feels Aunt Myrtle staring at him again. Her eyes are squinted and her mouth is turned down in a disapproving way. Slowly, Gavin puts down the chicken bone he was happily gnawing on. He wipes his hands on the napkin he has in his lap, picks up his knife and fork, and attempts to cut the chicken off the bone. Chicken just doesn't taste as good this way, but Aunt Myrtle is a firm believer in not eating with one's hands if it can be helped. Even though his mom doesn't mind it if it's a drumstick. Gavin sighs and moves on to the peas that he's been avoiding. They usually give him a gagging feeling. He stabs one pea with his fork and puts it in his mouth.

The nastiness is almost more than he can bear. He takes a deep breath. He doesn't dare gag in front of Aunt Myrtle. He puts another pea in his mouth, noting that Aunt Myrtle has continued to peer at him over her glasses.

"Why are you eating your food like that? One pea at a time?"

Before Gavin can think of an answer, Danielle says, "He always eats his peas like that, Aunt Myrtle. He doesn't like peas."

"I didn't ask you," Aunt Myrtle says, turning to Danielle. "I asked Gavin here."

Gavin almost smiles, but he holds it back. "I can get them down better this way."

"Well, that's just nonsense. Eat those peas. I want to see you take a forkful and eat them down. Right now."

Gavin feels his face grow warm. He holds his breath and swallows hard. There's no way he can take a whole forkful of peas, put them in his mouth, chew, and then *swallow*. That's just impossible. Usually he eats a pea or two at a time. Sometimes he can manage to eat half a forkful if he takes a quick gulp of milk to get it down.

He begins to click his teeth, which is what he does when he gets nervous, like when a scary scene in a movie is just about to get scarier.

"I'm waiting," Aunt Myrtle says.

His mom and dad exchange looks, but he can't tell if they're about to jump in or not. They seem to be waiting as well.

Danielle, on the other hand, has a sly smile on her lips. She watches him with one eyebrow raised. She even stops eating, as if to focus all her attention on his misery.

Gavin scoops up a few peas with his fork.

"That's not a forkful," Aunt Myrtle says.

Gavin looks over at his mother. He can't read her face. He can't tell if she approves or disapproves of what Aunt Myrtle is making him do. His father, however, is going about eating his dinner. Gavin scoops up a full forkful. He looks at it as if the peas are his personal enemy. Slowly, he places the fork in his mouth. He feels a gag starting up at the back of his throat. Totally out of his control, he feels a lurch in his stomach. His eyes grow big with alarm. Quickly, he grabs his glass of milk and takes a huge swig and then another. The peas go down. He breathes a big sigh of relief and looks

over at Aunt Myrtle. The corners of
her mouth have sunk down even
further.

"I think you've spoiled this
boy, Lisa," she says to his mom.
It always sounds strange when
someone calls his mother by her
first name. He thinks of his parents' names: *Lisa and Greg.* Like they're
regular people, and not his and Danielle's mom and dad.

"Yes, I think this boy's been allowed to get away with
things."

"Like what, Aunt Myrtle?" his mother asks with a
strange tone in her voice.

"Why, look what he allowed that little friend of his to do
to Danielle's prized souvenir."

Now Danielle really perks up. She'd met Aunt Myrtle at
the door with her dumb tale of woe about that stupid snow
globe. She'd even squeezed out a few tears. She knows she's
Aunt Myrtle's favorite. *Kiss-up!* Gavin thinks.

"Why, I think Gavin here should pay his sister what that
thing cost."

"We were considering that," Gavin's mom says.

Danielle shifts in her seat. She can hardly contain herself.

"When I move in next week, I'll let him walk Carlotta. It'll be his little job, to learn the value of a dollar." She sits back in her chair, pleased with her plan. "Yes, I need someone to walk Carlotta, and he needs to *earn* the money to replace that snow globe. We'll give him two dollars a day, which is really too much to walk a dog, but comes out of the goodness of my heart."

Several things make Gavin's brows sink: *move in* and *little job* and *two* measly *dollars*? What's all this about Aunt Myrtle moving in? And walking Carlotta, that mean, snarling dog of hers, is going to be his *job*, for just two dollars a day? Well, it's better than a quarter a day, he supposes.

As if she's heard some of his unspoken questions, Gavin's mom turns to Danielle and Gavin and says, "Aunt Myrtle is going to stay with us for a week or so while Uncle Vestor goes to his Barbershop Harmonizers' Convention in Kansas City."

Gavin looks over at Uncle Vestor, who's now smiling,

with a faraway expression on his face. He looks like a man who's getting ready to make a great escape.

"So," his mother continues, "since Auntie doesn't like to stay in their big house all alone, I thought it might be nice if she stayed here." Mom smiles brightly at each of them. Danielle cocks her head and smiles back. Gavin stares down at his hands.

"Isn't this good news?" his mother prods. "Aren't we going to be happy to have her? Especially you, Gavin. Now you're going to have this nice little way to earn money and show responsibility."

"I don't know if my snow globe can actually be *replaced*," Danielle says — just to complicate things, Gavin suspects.

"Well," Aunt Myrtle says, "he'll be able to give you its value." She turns back to Gavin. "Now, let's eat those peas."

Why did he think Aunt Myrtle would forget about the peas? Why would he think that he could somehow get out of finishing them off? Once again, he must struggle with another forkful with all eyes on him. He holds his breath and manages to get it down by thinking of the peach cobbler his mother made for dessert. *Mind over matter.* As soon as his audience has moved their attention away from him and onto their own concerns, he manages to deposit the next forkful into the napkin on his lap. He looks up just as Aunt Myrtle is mentioning Carlotta's accommodations.

His mom doesn't like dogs in the house, and that's going to be a problem. "We have a nice little shed off the garage, Aunt Myrtle," she says now.

Aunt Myrtle's mouth presses into a disapproving line, and she looks to Gavin's dad. In a quiet voice she says, "Carlotta is not an outside dog. The shock would probably kill her."

Gavin drops his head down to hide the smile he's trying very hard not to show.

Aunt Myrtle goes on. "The only time she's ever outside is when Vestor here walks her."

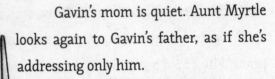

Gavin's mom is quiet. Aunt Myrtle looks again to Gavin's father, as if she's addressing only him.

This seems to force his dad to take a stand. "I think we can keep Carlotta on the back porch behind a child's gate. We still have the one we used when Gavin was little in the garage."

Gavin's mom doesn't say anything.

She takes a bite of mashed potatoes. Aunt Myrtle smiles as if she's just won a boxing-match round.

When the last of his peas have either been washed down with milk or slipped into his napkin — which he plans to stuff into his pocket and discard in the toilet at the first opportunity — Gavin asks to be excused. He has to do this only when Aunt Myrtle and Uncle Vestor are visiting. Before his mother can answer, Aunt Myrtle checks his plate. She squints at it for a few seconds as if trying to find a pea. "You may go," she finally says.

He stands, quickly shoves his balled-up napkin into his pocket, and practically backs out of the room. He's free! However, before he can completely escape the dining room, Aunt Myrtle gets in, "Gavin here is going to make a good dog walker while Vestor is at his Harmonizers' Convention. I know he and Carlotta are going to get along just fine."

Gavin manages to smile weakly. He thinks of Carlotta's face, the round black button nose, the ugly cotton-candy orange feathery fur with bits of black and white, those short little legs and sharp toenails that make clicking noises on hard floors. He thinks of Carlotta's mouth, always fixed in something between a grin and a leer while she pants her stinky breath and shows off her pointed razor-sharp canines as if she'd love to sink them into Gavin's leg. Her liquidy eyes are always bright and menacing. A week with Carlotta . . . How will he ever be able to stand it?

Three
Problems, Problems, Problems

Without Gavin having any say whatsoever, the details of his "little job" are arranged. The next morning at breakfast, he finds out all about it. They are sitting at the table, and Danielle is pouring the last bit of juice into her glass all the way up to the brim as she laughs to herself. He ignores her and protests, "Danielle took all the juice."

"Hmm?" his father says. He's reading the newspaper and sipping his coffee, and Gavin knows he's not really listening. Then he hears tiny clicks on the hall tiles growing louder, coming toward the kitchen. Next, Gavin hears Aunt Myrtle's voice. "Careful with that, Vestor. Oh, just take my cases on upstairs." Then Carlotta rounds the corner and stands expectantly in the kitchen doorway, panting, her little face surrounded by grotesque orange fur that looks prickly enough to cut someone. She stares at Gavin, then one side of her thin black dog lip curls up and Gavin hears a low, throaty sound.

"Now, don't do that, Carlotta." Aunt Myrtle cluck-clucks and reaches down to scoop the dog up in her arms. She tickles her stomach and coos. "There's my baby," she says, pursing her lips.

Gavin wants to gag. It's almost worse than eating peas. His mother appears and ushers Aunt Myrtle to the area behind the child's gate that's blocking off the back porch.

"Here, Auntie. This is what we have set up for Carlotta." Aunt Myrtle looks over at the straw basket where Gavin's mom usually keeps newspapers. It has been nicely lined with an old baby quilt. She sniffs and gives Carlotta a squeeze as if to protect her. She sits down at the table — with Carlotta! Gavin's eyes grow big as he looks from his mother to Aunt Myrtle and then back to his mother again. His mother turns to his father with an expression on her face that Gavin knows is a cry for help.

Gavin can feel his father sighing to himself. He gets up, walks over to his aunt, and gently takes Carlotta from her arms. "I'm sure Carlotta is going to like her new quarters," he says. He places the dog on her new bed on the back porch. Carlotta scratches at the quilt for a few moments, then settles down with her head resting on her paws. She looks at Aunt Myrtle as if pleading her case. Aunt Myrtle, her mouth set in a grim line, says, "I'd like some tea, please. That is, if you have tea."

"Of course." Gavin's mom jumps up to turn on the burner under the kettle.

This is what Gavin learns from Aunt Myrtle while she sips her tea: She isn't hungry for anything else. Gavin will walk Carlotta once a day, after school, so he must come home right away. No messing around. If — and this is a big "if" — he performs his job satisfactorily, Aunt Myrtle will pay him enough to replace Danielle's snow globe with something like it.

"Though I know you can't replace the exact snow globe," Aunt Myrtle adds, looking over at Danielle with sympathy.

"I got that snow globe in New York City at the choir fest," Danielle says.

Gavin rolls his eyes. He doesn't believe for a minute that Danielle is still all that sad about that dumb snow globe. She's just happy about his troubles, Gavin is sure. He looks over at Carlotta. She's up on her short little legs turning around and around on the folded quilt. It would be so much better if she were a real dog — something way bigger, something that could be a true friend. At least Carlotta is ignoring him and not giving him mean, threatening looks — for now.

● ● ●

When Gavin enters the classroom of his new school, Carver Elementary, he sees that his teacher, Ms. Shelby-Ortiz (who does not know how great he is at times tables, soccer, and skateboarding) has assigned *Problems, Problems, Problems* as the morning journal topic. He stares at it. Then he thinks about Ms. Shelby-Ortiz's two names. He'd heard one of the bossy girls, Deja, explain to her friend Nikki that modern women, up-to-date women, like keeping their own names now — the names they grew up with. Nowadays, Deja had said, women don't have to have their husband's name at all, and that's the way she's going to do it. When she grows up, she's going to keep her own last name. Or stick it together with her husband's name, just like Ms. Shelby-Ortiz. Gavin doesn't know if he likes that Deja girl. She reminds him too much of his sister, Danielle.

Other kids are staring at the morning journal topic too. Richard, the cause of Gavin's troubles, isn't even bothering to look at it. Gavin can see he's playing with some rubbery thing in his desk. Danielle would call Richard a knucklehead. From Gavin's seat behind him, he gets a pretty good view of the array of toys Richard brings to school.

Ms. Shelby-Ortiz seems pleased with the topic she's come up with. She smiles encouragingly at all the students who are getting ready to write. "I chose this topic because I realized that life is like math. How is it like math, class?"

Oh, no, Gavin thinks. He hopes that she doesn't start calling on kids and get around to him. Because he definitely doesn't know how life is like math.

"Two points for the table of the student who tells me how life is like math."

Ms. Shelby-Ortiz has them sitting at cooperative groups of four desks, which she calls tables. They are competing all week. Then on Friday, the winning table earns a big gold star on the Winners' Board. At the end of the month, the students at the winning table get to put their hands in the grab bag and extract a reward. And they aren't cheesy things like pencils and erasers, they're different kinds of prizes, like small magnifying glasses, kaleidoscopes that can fit in your pocket, and min-iature tic-tac-toe sets.

Now the hands begin to fly up. Suddenly, Gavin knows exactly how life is like math. And he just bets that most of the answers the other kids are going to give aren't going to make sense. *And* there's going to be a bunch of people who don't even have an answer but are raising their hands anyway. He might as well put an end to this right now. He raises his hand too, but Ms. Shelby-Ortiz is busy giving some of the knuckleheads a chance.

"Because it takes three hundred and sixty-five days to get through a year?" Ralph calls out.

Ms. Shelby Ortiz looks at him for a moment. "Nooo," she says slowly, frowning just a tiny little bit. Then she looks over at Richard, who's uncharacteristically raising his hand with a calm look on his face. She calls on him and cocks her head challengingly.

"Because you all the time have to be solving problems, just like in math."

Gavin feels himself deflate a little bit. That's just what he was going to say. And he thought he was the only one thinking of it.

Ms. Shelby-Ortiz looks especially thrilled. "That's right, Richard," she says, beaming. "That's exactly right, class.

Think about it. In life, you solve one problem after another. No one's life is problem-free. So I want you to think of a problem that you have right now and how you plan to solve it. Let's have some input before you begin to write." She looks around at all of them. Gavin looks around too. Some kids still look puzzled. Others look eager to begin.

"Who wants to go first?"

That stuck-up girl, Antonia, raises her hand. Ms. Shelby-Ortiz calls on her. "Yes, Antonia."

"I have a problem to solve."

"Go ahead. Tell us what it is."

"My grandmother is coming for a visit. She always brings me a gift that . . ." She pauses, searching for the right words. "I don't like her presents. They're *never* anything I like. I want to ask her to skip the present and just give me the money that she would have spent instead."

Gavin sees Ms. Shelby-Ortiz's face go from interested to puzzled. Her lips even part in amazement.

"Antonia, that would be rude. No one gives gifts to cause displeasure or unhappiness. When someone gives you a gift, they're trying really hard to make you happy. If you say that to her, your grandmother will look back on all the gifts she's given you over the years and think that perhaps you never liked even one of them. You can't solve your problem by hurting someone's feelings."

Gavin can't tell how Antonia feels about this. She looks thoughtful, like she's planning on not following Ms. Shelby-Ortiz's advice — like she's going to put her plan into action anyway. Antonia's probably thinking that she, Antonia, knows best.

"Class," Ms. Shelby-Ortiz says, "I'm sure you know what I want you to do, so let's get started."

Why do teachers always say "let's" and "we" and "our," like they have to do the assignment too, when they don't? Gavin thinks. It's just something he wonders. He opens his journal, which has a lot of blank pages, since he's new to the school. On the cover is his name written by the teacher in neat block letters. He puts the date in the upper right corner of the page just like Ms. Shelby-Ortiz has instructed the class to do. Of course there are those who have to be told to do this every day. Gavin wonders about them, too. Then he dives in:

> I have a problem. The beginning of this problem
> wasn't even my fault. It was this other guy's

fault. Richard. He got me in trouble on Saturday.
He broke my sister's spechal sno-globe, and now
I have to walk this horrible dog to get money to
pay for it. She cant even get a exact copy because
she got that sno-globe in New York not here. Now
I have to walk this ugly dog every day. A dog
that's all the time giving me mean looks and showing
her teeth and looking like she would like to bite me.
I have to be with this dog every day. Which is too
much. And my aunt, who's really my dad's aunt, will
probably give me just a dollar for all my work.
I wish this was the last problem Im going to
have in my whole life, but it probably wont be.

Gavin reads over what he's written. He likes it. He's just in time, because Ms. Shelby-Ortiz orders the whole class to stop writing. She has a girl named Rosario collect the journals. Knowing that the teacher's going to read it, he goes back over it in his mind. Yeah, he decides. He likes what he's written. He hands it over with pride.

● ● ●

"Did you get in trouble?" Richard asks as they walk to the sock-ball area on the schoolyard.

"Yeah, I got in trouble. Now I have to take care of my

great-aunt's dog to earn money to give to my annoying sister."

"That's not so bad," Richard says.

"Not for you," Gavin says.

"But I said, 'Catch.'"

Gavin doesn't know why Richard keeps saying that. "You said, 'Catch,' as you were throwing it. I didn't have time to get my hands up."

"Well, can you go skateboarding after school?"

"I told you, I have to walk my great-aunt's dog."

"What's a great-aunt?"

"It's the aunt of your mother or your father."

Richard gives this some thought. "Then she must be really old, huh?"

"Yeah, she's pretty old," Gavin agrees.

"I know," Richard says. "I'll help you."

Gavin thinks about this. Just how much help will Richard be? Not much, he decides, but still, he wouldn't mind the company. "Okay," he says. "Come to my house at about four." Gavin plans to have his snack first before taking Carlotta out. He always comes home from school starved.

Four
On the Job, Day One

As Gavin moseys up his front walkway, the door opens, and there stands Aunt Myrtle with Queen Carlotta in her arms all dolled up in a big pink satin bow somehow clipped to the fur on top of her head. She wears a little lace sweater and a rhinestone collar spelling out her name. There's no way in the world he can walk that silly-looking dog without getting laughed at. He's new to the neighborhood. What's that going to look like? There's just no way.

"We've been waiting for the last forty minutes," Aunt Myrtle says, starting right in. "Were you dilly-dallying?" First of all, Gavin's not sure he knows just what *dilly-dallying* is. He guesses it means fooling around and wasting time.

"No, Aunt Myrtle. I came right home."

She steps aside to let him pass. He can tell she's annoyed. Even the mutt, as Gavin thinks of her, lets out a quick, snappish bark of complaint. "Well, Carlotta's ready for her walk. Let me explain a few things to you." Aunt Myrtle turns and walks down the hall to the kitchen. Gavin wonders where his mother is. Probably at the store. Then Aunt Myrtle lets Carlotta spill out of her arms, and immediately the dog begins its yap-yapping and runs in tight circles around Gavin's ankles. He tries to step out of the way before he feels the first nips.

"Carlotta!" Aunt Myrtle says. "Sit!" Carlotta sinks down onto her belly, but then begins to scoot stealthily toward Gavin, who hurries to the other side of the table. *She must be a demon dog,* he thinks.

"Look here," says Aunt Myrtle. "This is Carlotta's leash. Carlotta is a very good dog. She's had special training." Carlotta has stopped scooting and now seems to be trying to clean her nose with her pink tongue. "But keep her on her leash at all times. I want you to walk her to the park and then back here. That should be long enough." Aunt Myrtle reaches into her sweater pocket and pulls out a plastic bag. She hands it to Gavin.

"What's this for?" he asks.

"Why, it's for when Carlotta does her business."

"Her business?" Gavin has a sinking feeling. There's something about that term, *her business,* that he doesn't like.

"When she does number two."

"Number two?" Gavin repeats, scrunching up his face.

"Yes, number two. That's why you're taking her out. So she can do her business." Aunt Myrtle gives a short, vigorous nod.

"Number *two?*" *Where's Mom?* Gavin wonders again. Why isn't she there to rescue him?

"Number two goes in this plastic bag, and then you throw it away in the can outside when you get back."

"Yeah," Danielle says, slithering into the kitchen. She goes to the refrigerator and takes out a carton of yogurt. "Make sure you don't throw it in the kitchen trash." She gives Gavin a fake smile, then pirouettes and leaves as fast as she's come.

Aunt Myrtle has attached Queen Carlotta to her leash. She hands it to Gavin and has him walk back and forth across the kitchen until she's satisfied he can handle the responsibility. Then she gives him a list of instructions. "I need you to read the instructions I've written out loud so

I can make sure you understand what you need to know about walking Carlotta."

Aunt Myrtle has written her instructions in cursive. Gavin just started learning cursive at the beginning of the school year. Ms. Shelby-Ortiz often has to rewrite stuff in manuscript because too many kids are still having trouble reading cursive. Plus Aunt Myrtle's handwriting is really scribbly.

"Go ahead," she says, sounding kind of impatient.

"It's hard to read . . . your handwriting."

"Oh, for Pete's sake!" Aunt Myrtle sighs heavily. "Now, you listen carefully. Number One: This is a retractable leash. You mustn't give Carlotta too much leash or too little. Best to let it have a little bit of a dip."

Gavin has no idea what that means, but he's not going to ask her to explain. He just wants to get this chore over with as fast as possible. "Okay," he says.

"Number Two: If you see another dog — say, a dangerous-looking big dog — you make sure you keep Carlotta safe, even if you have to pick her up." She looks at Gavin warily. "Do you understand?"

"Yes, Aunt Myrtle." He actually doesn't know what he'll do in a situation like that, but he nods in agreement.

"Number Three: Walk Carlotta for thirty minutes. Check your watch. When you've walked fifteen minutes one way, it's time to turn around and walk back home. I don't want to be sitting here worried."

"Yes, Aunt Myrtle," he says again, wondering how long this is going to go on.

"Now, come on over to the table."

In the middle of it is a bowl of fruit. Aunt Myrtle takes an apple and places it on the table. "Give me that plastic bag."

Gavin hands it over.

"This is how you pick up Carlotta's business."

Gavin frowns at the apple. Then he looks down at Carlotta, who is busy sniffing the floor around the table for crumbs. He feels a growing horror. Never had he thought about Carlotta going to the bathroom . . . *that* way.

Aunt Myrtle continues with her instruction. "Now, this is what you do." She puts her hand in the bag, then places it over the apple. She picks up the apple, holds it high, then pulls the bag inside out by grabbing its top edge with her other hand. She gives the top end a twist and then ties the twisted end into a knot. "Simple," she says. "And it's the law."

Not simple! Gavin cries out in his mind. He's going to gag. He knows he will.

"And make sure she has plenty of sniff time. A dog needs sniff time. Even if you have to be out longer than thirty minutes."

Aunt Myrtle pushes him out the door, then stands at the window watching him. He can feel her eyes on his back. He spots Richard heading his way. What a relief. Since it's because of Richard that he's in this mess, maybe Richard will take care of the *dirty work*.

"Come on," Gavin says to the horrible dog at his feet.

● ● ●

Carlotta, in her lace and bow, is almost impossible to walk. Either she runs ahead, pulling at the leash, or she stops to sniff at something on someone's lawn. Right in the middle of walking at a halfway decent pace, she has to backtrack and get some sniffs in on something she might have missed. *Why do dogs sniff so much?* Gavin wonders. And Richard's no help either. His mind is on this new video game he played over at Carlos's. He's telling Gavin all about it. At one point, he offers, "You shoulda brought some dog treats or something." Gavin sighs at the useless advice.

Then there are the times Carlotta dashes in circles, wrapping the leash around his legs as she goes.

"Man, that dog is crazy," Richard says with a mouth full of potato chips. He watches Gavin untangle himself. If Gavin had gotten his way, he would be eating his special snack of wheat crackers and grape jam at home right now. Ten little wheat crackers with grape jam spread on each one and a tall, cold glass of chocolate milk. His mouth waters just thinking about it.

"Want some chips?" Richard asks, angling the bag at him. Then he notices the plastic bag in Gavin's hand. "Whatcha got that for?"

"For Carlotta's business."

"Her what?"

"When she goes to the bathroom."

"She goes in that bag?"

Gavin looks at Richard, puzzled. He tries to imagine what Richard has in mind. The picture is ridiculous. "No, Richard. I have this bag for when Carlotta goes to the bathroom on somebody's grass. I pick it up with my hand in this bag and then throw it away in the outside can when I get back."

Richard takes this in with no response. Then suddenly he cries out, "Eeeew!" He looks over at Gavin, his eyes huge. "Eeeew! You have to do that?"

"It's the law," Gavin says grimly.

Richard peers down at Carlotta, prancing and straining at her leash. "Ugh," he says.

Gavin glances down and then up at three boys from the fifth grade at the end of the block, heading their way. It's Richard's older brother Darnell and two of his friends, Gregory Johnson and that big boy with the last name for a first name — Harper, who's way too big to be in fifth grade. He's one of the other new students, and someone said he was in third grade twice. There's something about him that Gavin doesn't like.

Maybe their paths won't cross, Gavin hopes. The older boys are walking super slowly, and every once in a while they stop to pretend they're playing an imaginary basketball game.

Gavin looks down at Carlotta again. His heart sinks as he takes in the pink bow, the lace sweater, and the rhinestone collar. It can't get much worse.

Plus he's got a pink leash in one hand and that plastic bag in the other hand. Anyone with a dog will know what *that's* for. What would be really good right now is if the sidewalk would open up so he could drop down into an underground tunnel. He feels some big laughter coming his way.

"Hey," Richard says, "there's Darnell and them."

Gavin turns, pulling on Carlotta's leash as he changes direction. "Let's go this way," he says. But Richard is already waving his hands over his head like he's a referee on a football field and calling out his brother's name.

"Hey, Darnell!"

"Oh, no. No, no, no," Gavin says under his breath as he sees all the boys' attention suddenly directed at them. He watches them stop and begin to point and laugh. Now they seem to have forgotten their pretend basketball game. They're making their way toward Gavin, Richard, and . . . *Carlotta*. If only he could disappear. Of course, Richard doesn't get it. He's busy encouraging them.

"What are you guys doing? Where you going?"

Suddenly, Carlotta races around Gavin until he's practically bound up in the leash again. This brings more laughter from the three older boys.

"That your dog?" Darnell asks Gavin, elbowing Harper.

"No, it's his aunt's," Richard says, watching Gavin struggle to untangle himself from the leash.

"What kind of dog is that?" Darnell asks. His lip curls with disdain. "And why'd you put that bow in its fur?"

"I didn't put that bow in its fur," Gavin says, horrified that anyone would think such a thing. He shortens the leash, and Carlotta strains against it. Then, of course, she starts up with her shrill, annoying yapping. "She's a Pomeranian," Gavin adds.

"Why do you have a *Pomeranian?*" Darnell asks, frowning. "What good is a *Pomeranian?* It's like you don't even have a real dog."

"This is *not* my dog," Gavin says, feeling his face grow hot. "I just have to walk it."

"And pick up dog doo," Darnell adds, noticing the plastic bag. He begins to laugh, extra loudly, until he gets his friends joining in.

Then Richard starts laughing. Richard, who's supposed to be Gavin's friend. Gavin decides to ignore everybody and move on past them. He starts toward Marin, but he can hear their taunting voices mixed with loud laughter at his back all the way down the street.

"Hey, Gavin! Where you going?" Darnell calls out. "Come on back. We didn't mean to hurt your feelings!" But Darnell

can hardly get that out before he breaks down laughing again.

Then that Harper guy says, "We understand. You can't help it if you love your little Pommermaniac!" Everyone bursts out laughing at his joke: Darnell, Gregory Johnson, and Richard. Harper laughs loudest.

Gavin keeps walking, his mouth pinched with determination to ignore the laughter.

When he turns onto Marin, the voices finally fade. Then there's just him and Carlotta. Richard has gone off with the fifth-graders.

● ● ●

Luckily for Gavin, Carlotta has had no "business" to deposit on anyone's front lawn so far. And walking down Marin is kind of nice. There's a bike shop with big motorcycles lining the sidewalk. Then there's a doughnut shop with the most wonderful aroma wafting out of it. He plans to bring money tomorrow and buy a couple, then eat them in front of Danielle and make her drool. He can't wait. Then there's the hobby store, with all kinds of interesting stuff in the window. Little Miss Carlotta is prancing along, all happy, it seems, and Gavin is thinking, *This isn't so bad.* They pass the coffee shop, and some of the customers are sitting at outdoor tables, sipping their drinks, chatting with one another or just checking out the happenings on Marin.

This is not bad at all. Four more days of this and he'll have earned the money for Danielle's snow globe. Uncle Vestor will be back from his conference, and things will be back to normal. No more Aunt Myrtle checking his plate to see if he's eaten all his Brussels sprouts or beans or turnip greens.

They pass Wendy's Wonderful Wigs with its crazy display of wigs on a stand just outside the store. Blond ones, red ones, brown ones, and jet-black. Suddenly, Carlotta begins that low, throaty sound she makes when she's thinking about misbehaving. It gives Gavin a not-so-good feeling. He clutches the leash a little tighter in anticipation of — what, he doesn't know. He looks down at Carlotta. Something about the way she's pulling a little at the leash fills him with dread. He needs to get her past Wendy's Wonderful Wigs. There's something about the place that's disturbing her. He could cross the street. But no, he's too far from the corner traffic light. It would be dangerous.

He decides to go the other way, but Carlotta lurches forward, throwing her whole body into the move with surprising strength. The leash jerks out of his hand, and Carlotta makes a mad dash toward the display of wigs. Helplessly, Gavin watches her leap at a blond wig cut into the shape of Moe's hair from *The Three Stooges*. Carlotta lets out a low growl while shaking the wig vigorously.

"Stop that dog!" a voice behind Gavin shrieks. Could it be Wendy of Wendy's Wonderful Wigs? She toddles out in some of the highest heels he's ever seen. She throws her hands in the air and does a little hop on her high, high heels. "Stop that dog!" she repeats, then looks around for help. The butcher has come out of his shop next door. While Gavin looks on, not knowing what to do, the butcher grabs one end of the wig and begins to pull. But Carlotta's got an iron grip on it. She curls her lips back, showing her teeth clenched tightly on the wig as she hangs on furiously. Gavin never knew that Carlotta could be so strong — and stubborn. He knows he should do something, but he can only stand there watching.

Finally, with one strong jerk, the butcher frees the wig and holds it up out of Carlotta's reach. Gavin manages to grab the leash and wind the end around his hand just as Carlotta leaps up at the wig again.

"That's a dangerous dog!" the wig lady screams. She stands there holding her head as if she has a terrible headache. "She should not be allowed out if she can't be controlled!"

"I'm really sorry, ma'am. I didn't know she didn't like wigs. I just started walking this dog today. She's not even my dog."

With that, Gavin shortens the leash even more. Carlotta struggles against it. He has to practically drag her away from the shop and its enticing wig stand. All the way down the street, Carlotta tries to pull back toward Wendy's Wonderful Wigs, as if she just wants one more go at that blond wig. The end of the block seems miles away. He hears the wig lady's protests at his back until he finally turns the corner toward his house.

Then, as if that isn't enough, Queen Carlotta starts barking at a big Labrador snoozing in the shade of an elm tree in a fenced yard. She must know that there's no way the big dog can get at her, because she turns ferocious, pulling back her lips, snarling and barking loudly, and straining in the

Labrador's direction until the big dog is furiously running back and forth on the other side of the fence, barking in frustration.

"Cut it out!" Gavin yells as he pulls her away. "Leave that dog alone!" But Carlotta, still proving her bravery, pulls the other way. That's when he decides he's had enough. He scoops her up and practically runs the rest of the way home.

Of course, Aunt Myrtle is at the door waiting for him. Her brow is furrowed and her hand is on her chest.

"I've been so worried," she says in a breathless voice. "Might I remind you, you were to walk her thirty minutes total? It's been a good forty minutes."

Gavin's shoulders sink. He doesn't see all that much difference between thirty minutes and forty. And anyway, didn't Aunt Myrtle tell him to give Carlotta plenty of sniff time?

Then Aunt Myrtle spots the empty plastic bag in Gavin's hand.

"You're bringing back that bag empty? You should have stayed out longer."

Gavin looks up at his great-aunt. He opens his mouth to speak, but he truly can't think of anything to say. He can't win.

Five
Where's Carlotta's Chew-Chew?

As soon as Gavin walks onto the schoolyard the next morning, he sees Richard on the basketball court playing one-on-one with his brother Darnell. Gavin walks the other way toward the handball courts. When he gets there, he just sits on the bench and watches the handball game in progress. He's a little irritated about Richard's lack of loyalty from the afternoon before. He can still hear his loud laughter. He just might not talk to Richard for a while. Maybe he'll find a new friend. He glances over at the basketball court and sighs.

Richard catches his eye then and waves him over. But Gavin stays put as if he doesn't even see him. Richard throws the ball to his brother and runs over to the handball court. He straddles the bench where Gavin sits with his elbow resting on his knee.

"What's up?" Richard asks.

Gavin looks off across the yard. "Nothin'."

"How come you're over here and not playing with us?"

"I don't feel like it."

Richard stares at Gavin for a moment, then says, "You look like you're mad about something."

"Why would I be mad about something?"

"Is it because I didn't finish walking that dog with you? I had to go."

"Right."

"For real. I had some chores I had to do at home."

Gavin shrugs. The freeze bell rings. Almost everyone freezes in place. Except Harper. He's busy rolling a basketball around with his foot. *Some kids just have to break rules no matter what*, Gavin thinks. When the second bell rings, Gavin gets up and walks to Room Ten's line. Richard follows.

● ● ●

"Can you get permission to come to the skate park?" Richard asks as they skip down the steps after school. He'd been acting extra nice to Gavin throughout the day, even giving him his pudding cup at lunch. Some of Gavin's anger has drifted away. "I'm gonna run home and get my skateboard and something to eat, and then I'm going to the skate park with Darnell and his friends," Richard continues.

"I have to walk Carlotta. Remember?" Gavin says, annoyed that Richard needs reminding.

"Oh, yeah." Richard seems to be mulling this over. "What about after you walk Carlotta?"

"Then it's time to do my homework. But I'll see."

So of course, as Gavin walks home — alone, since Richard has run off to the skate park to meet his brother and his brother's friends — he rehearses how he'll put this question to his mom. He's not all that hopeful. His mother can be pretty strict about homework.

But as far as Carlotta's concerned, his plan is all mapped out. He's going nowhere *near* that wig place. Then he has an idea, an even better plan that will take care of his obligation to that furry fiend while letting him have some fun. After all, it isn't his fault that Danielle's snow globe got broken. Sure, he shouldn't have been in her room — but then, she shouldn't be keeping candy in her room to tempt him. Anybody would be tempted. Anybody!

Gavin practically bounces up his front porch steps, anxious to drop his backpack by the staircase inside and hurry into the kitchen to make his snack. He'll even remember to wash his hands. Then when his mother calls out, "Don't forget to wash your hands," he can say, "I already did." He loves beating his mom to the punch. "Put your backpack on the bottom step, out of the way," she's always saying. "I already did," he'll be able to call back. But now that Aunt Myrtle's here, it seems his mother suddenly has a lot to do, away from home — a lot of volunteer work and stuff. And his dad doesn't get home until six. That leaves Gavin at the mercy of Danielle and Aunt Myrtle. What a duo!

He's still imagining the way his snack time will go when the door swings open and Aunt Myrtle appears with Carlotta in her arms before he can even climb the porch steps.

"There you are," she snaps. "You take Carlotta, and I'll take your backpack." She puts Carlotta, already attached to the pink leash, down on the porch. Gavin hands over his backpack and takes the plastic bag and leash. This is the second day in a row he didn't get to have his wheat crackers and grape jam! Sometimes he thinks grownups forget that kids have feelings too. How would Aunt Myrtle like it if she was hungry and somebody gave her a big chore to do before she could even eat? She probably wouldn't like it at all.

"Oh," Aunt Myrtle says, pulling a rawhide bone from her pocket. "Don't forget to take Carlotta's Chew-Chew." Aunt Myrtle nuzzles Carlotta's mouth with the special little bone that Carlotta is always playing with or attacking with her sharp little teeth. It's her favorite thing in all the world — according to Aunt Myrtle. "When she gets sidetracked sniffing at everything, just coax her away with this."

Gavin takes the grubby thing out of her hand, trying to put the thought of all the dried dog spit that it's probably covered with out of his mind. The end of the week can't come soon enough.

"That's okay," he says to himself under his breath as he ambles down the front walkway. He has a plan. "Aunt Myrtle," he says, stopping at the sidewalk and looking back, "can I keep Carlotta out a little longer? I think she really likes to be out."

Aunt Myrtle squints and purses her lips, thinking this over. "I guess it won't hurt. But no more than an hour."

"Yes, ma'am," Gavin says. He hears the door close behind him, and instead of heading down Willow Avenue, his own street, he walks up his driveway to the backyard. His skateboard and helmet are there, propped up against the side of the house. He can't get to his kneepads and elbow pads, because they're up in his room. He'll just have to do without them. He has no intention of letting Miss Carlotta the Curse ruin his life.

Too bad he didn't think of this yesterday. He feels pretty good with his skateboard under his arm, his helmet dangling from his free hand, and Carlotta prancing along beside him. She's actually being really good. Gavin thinks she's going to love the park, anyway. Maybe she's picking up his excitement and she's excited too. He once read that dogs are supposed to be kind of sensitive, able to pick up moods and stuff.

As soon as he spots the special fenced-off skate park with its steep slopes and curved walls and stairs and railings and bowl's edges, Gavin's stomach flutters with anticipation. His feet are itching to jump on his board, but first he has to find a place to tie up Carlotta. It won't be so bad for her. Carlotta will have fun just looking at all the stuff going on in the park. Kids running around, dogs on the jogging path with their owners, soccer practice. Gavin's plan is to stay thirty minutes — no more. Ten minutes to get there, thirty minutes at the park, ten minutes to get back home. Another day down, four dollars in his account. He looks around. Not far away is one of those racks for chaining up a bike. It's only about ten feet from the skate park. Perfect.

Gavin marches Carlotta over to it, but when they get about three feet away, she begins to pull back. It's as if she knows this is it for her. It's like when his mother picks him up after school and he gets a funny feeling, but she waits until he's already in the car before she tells him, "Oh, yeah, you have an appointment at the dentist. That's where we're headed." Then he gets to think of that shot in the mouth all the way there.

He tugs at Carlotta's leash until he manages to get her to the bike rack. He loops it around the post and then ties a double knot. He tugs it until it's snug. All the while Carlotta is doing a little hop and pull, trying to free herself. He remembers her Chew-Chew and pulls it out of his pocket with just his thumb and fore-finger. It's so yucky, he holds it away from himself. He imagines that it was once white. Now it's a grungy gray with dark smudges that Gavin imagines are old drool. Gavin waves it in front of Carlotta's nose, hating that he has to touch the thing. She sniffs at it, but then looks at him with big sad eyes. He turns away and sees Richard on a bench just inside the chainlink fence that cordons off the skate area from the rest of the park. Carlotta starts up her yaps, and the sound follows him as he fast-walks over there.

Richard looks up and gives him a big grin of surprise. "I thought you had to walk that dog."

Gavin smiles slyly and points to Carlotta, who's settled down with her Chew-Chew. "I can only stay for a little bit. How come you're not skating?"

"'Cause that Harper guy has my skateboard. He said he just wanted to borrow it for five minutes, and it's been way longer than five minutes."

Gavin scans the skateboarders until he sees Harper on Richard's skateboard and Darnell on his own. He narrows his eyes, still a little angry about the day before. Gavin definitely doesn't like Harper. In fact, he feels Harper was the one who led the laughter at his expense.

"Is that guy your brother's good friend?"

"Kinda. They're in the same class, and he's always wanting to go everywhere Darnell goes and do whatever Darnell and his other friends are doing. He came from this other school. I bet you he got kicked out."

"Didn't he do third grade twice?"

Richard shrugs. "Maybe."

"Well, you can share my board. We can take turns."

Gavin slips on his helmet. He moves to the top of the first pocket and waits while one of the big boys goes down the curved wall, does a heel flip, propels himself up the opposite curved wall, then leaps onto the long stair railing. Down the older boy sails, like some kind of skateboard champion, to land nicely on top of his board, crouched and ready. Back and forth he goes, up and down one curved wall and then its opposite. It looks like he could do that forever.

Gavin can only do the curved walls. For now. He adjusts his helmet, and when there's an opening for him, he jumps on his board and skates the curved walls back and forth. It gives him a wonderful feeling of freedom. He loves it. He still has to learn all the tricks he sees the bigger boys doing all the time. As soon as he doesn't have this dog-sitting job anymore . . .

After a few minutes, he stops and carries his skateboard to Richard. He looks at Carlotta, who's going to town on her Chew-Chew. She's finally quieted down. She seems happy.

"Here you go," he says to Richard, handing over his board. Richard grins. He puts on his helmet and hurries off. Gavin watches him for a bit, then turns toward the more expert skateboarders. He can learn a lot just from observing them.

Gradually, Gavin becomes aware of a whimpering sound. At first, he pays no attention to it. The park is full of people and dogs. But little by little, the whimpering draws his attention away from the skateboarders. He glances over at Carlotta and sees her running back and forth, straining at her leash. She's making the strange whimpering noise, as if she's upset about something.

Gavin looks closely. He doesn't see Carlotta's Chew-Chew. He checks the ground all around her, but it's nowhere in sight. Where is it? "Richard," he calls out, "I have to see about Carlotta. Something's wrong."

Richard, who is standing on top of one of the big half-pipes and preparing to drop in, looks over at him and frowns.

"I have to go, anyway," Gavin shouts. "Just drop off my board at my house on your way home."

"Okay," Richard calls back. Gavin suspects his mind is already on his next maneuver.

● ● ●

Gavin searches the grass around Carlotta while she paces and whimpers. *It's got to be here,* he thinks. But it's not. Could a squirrel have gotten it and carried it off? He looks down at Carlotta and rolls his eyes. Because of this stupid dog, he's had to cut his fun short. He does feel a teensy bit sorry for her, though. Gavin tries petting Carlotta to calm her down, but it doesn't work. She just keeps whimpering, and now she's pulling at her leash. He leaves her tied to the bicycle rack and starts out in search of the Chew-Chew, keeping his eyes on the grass around him as he moves away.

He circles the soccer field with no luck, then heads toward the large climbing structure on the playground. Maybe one of the little kids ran off with it. Maybe his mother or father discovered that nasty thing in their child's possession and dropped it in the nearest garbage can. Gavin checks trash cans along the way. He grabs a thin branch from the ground and stirs the garbage around in each one. No Chew-Chew. He supposes he could dig down further, but it's getting late and he knows he should go get Carlotta and head home. He has a vision of Aunt Myrtle standing on the porch, scowling and tapping her foot.

As he starts for the next trash can on his way to the play structure, a large brown dog with long shaggy fur runs by. Its teeth are clamped down on something that looks just like Carlotta's Chew-Chew. In fact, he's sure it *is* Carlotta's Chew-Chew! It's the same grungy beige color. It has the same bitten-off ends ... The more he looks at it, the more he's sure. But ...

Suddenly he hears someone shout, "Whoa, Yankee! Get back here."

It's a big, tall boy who looks like he might be in high school, maybe even college. He's wearing a sweatshirt with some kind of school insignia on it. He has a deep, booming voice. "Now!" he yells.

Sheepishly, the dog stops, gives the Chew-Chew a fierce shake, then trots back to the tall boy. Carlotta's toy is still gripped between its teeth. The big guy ruffles the dog's fur and stoops to attach a leash to its collar. Gavin needs to get that Chew-Chew back. He takes in one big breath to gather his courage and starts off toward the high school (or college) guy, who looks up as Gavin approaches.

"Um, um . . ." Gavin starts.

The guy shades his eyes against the afternoon sun and looks down at him, but he doesn't say anything.

"Um . . . Your dog . . ."

"Yeah? What about him?"

Gavin tries to figure out if the guy's words are friendly or unfriendly. He looks from the dog to the owner and then back to the dog.

"What do you want?" the owner demands. That doesn't sound very friendly to Gavin.

He swallows. "I think your dog has my dog's . . . toy." Gavin's glad he left Carlotta tied up back at the skate park out of view. He'd be embarrassed if the guy thought Carlotta was *his* dog.

The guy looks down at the toy. "What makes you think so?"

Gavin gains a bit of courage and says, "When I got to the park, my dog had her . . ." He doesn't want to say *Chew-Chew*. It sounds dumb. ". . . *chew toy*. I mean, when I tied her up back at the skate park, she was playing with it. Now it's gone. And—"

The tall boy studies his dog. He seems to be thinking. Then he smiles. It's not a friendly smile. "Yeah. Yankee had that already. That's Yankee's."

Gavin doesn't know what to say. He knows the guy is lying. Gavin watches as he saunters away, his big brown dog by his side. It's not fair. The guy is bigger than Gavin. He's older. And that means one thing. The older, larger person can tell a giant fib and the smaller person can't do anything about it.

Gavin retraces his steps back to Carlotta, who is now jumping and yelping and making running attempts to free herself from the pole. He stands there and watches her for a moment. How is he going to explain her missing Chew-Chew? How? He can just see Aunt Myrtle's face when he tells her that a dog, *a big dog,* stole Carlotta's toy. Wait—he can't tell her that. He'll never hear the end of it from her. Aunt Myrtle will go on and on about Gavin not doing his job, not protecting Carlotta from losing her precious

Chew-Chew. She'll probably complain to his mother and father. She'll probably act like he lost some special treasure worth zillions of dollars. Danielle will love it. What is he going to do? He looks at the whining Carlotta. He scrunches his mouth to the side. This is not good.

Gavin paces back and forth. He can feel his heart beating fast while he thinks. He's got to come up with an idea. But what? For some reason Carlotta stops her fidgeting and looks up at him, as if she, too, is wondering what he's going to do. He unties her leash and starts home.

When he gets there, Gavin heads straight for the backyard. He hurries past the kitchen window, hoping Aunt Myrtle won't spot him. He has to think. He has to come up with an idea. It won't be long before she'll be cross-examining him about Carlotta's outing. That, of course, will lead her to notice the missing Chew-Chew.

"Give her to me," Aunt Myrtle says, startling Gavin, who'd been pacing again. He hadn't even heard her come out onto the back porch. Gavin climbs the stairs and hands her the leash. "How was everything?" Aunt Myrtle asks.

Gavin can smell something yucky cooking in the kitchen. His heart sinks. "It was okay," he says.

"Did she go to the bathroom?"

Oh, no, Gavin thinks. He'd forgotten all about that. Maybe she went to the bathroom while she was tied to the bike rack. But maybe she didn't. He can't be sure. Should he tell Aunt Myrtle a tiny fib? He can't just say that he doesn't know. "Uh, I don't think she had to go," he says.

"What? Again?" Aunt Myrtle frowns down at Carlotta. "I'm just going to have to change her kibble."

"Yeah, it must be the kibble," Gavin agrees.

Aunt Myrtle turns to go back into the kitchen, with Carlotta trotting behind her. Gavin heads straight to the kitchen sink to wash his hands — to wash all the school germs off his hands, as his mother says, and the dog germs, too. When he opens the cabinet to pull out the box of wheat crackers, Aunt Myrtle says, "What are you doing?"

"Um — I'm making me a snack."

Aunt Myrtle shakes her finger at Gavin. "No, too close to dinner," she proclaims.

He looks over at the stove. There's some awful stuff simmering in those pots. He just knows it. He closes the cabinet door and heads

for his room so he can drop off his backpack and maybe sneak in a video game or two before homework. He's almost out of the kitchen when Aunt Myrtle asks, "Where's Carlotta's Chew-Chew?"

Before Gavin can even think about what he's going to say, the words just come out. "I must have left it . . . *outside.*"

Aunt Myrtle looks over at Carlotta. She has settled onto her new bed on the porch with her head resting on her paws. "Well, you make sure you go get that Chew-Chew before the day is over. She has to have her Chew-Chew."

"Yes, Aunt Myrtle," Gavin says. He runs up the stairs. The door to Danielle's room is closed. She must be in there doing who knows what. His dad is still at work, and his mother must be at the market or something. The house is quiet. He slips into his room, closes the door, and breathes a sigh of relief.

Right in the middle of homework — right in the middle of writing ten declarative sentences and underlining the subject once and the predicate twice — Gavin gets his brilliant idea: *Just buy Carlotta another Chew-Chew.* He'll have to dip into the money he's been saving all year for a new skateboard, but anything is better than having to hear more of Aunt Myrtle's complaints.

Six
Harper and the Sticky Fingers

Ms. Shelby-Ortiz has written *Open Topic* on the white-board for their morning journal entries. Gavin doesn't know if he really likes *Open Topic*. He stares at the words for a minute. Then he looks around. Some kids, like him, are taking their time. Some, like that girl Nikki, have already dived in. He taps his pencil on the desk. Ms. Shelby-Ortiz looks over at him and he stops. He opens his journal and puts the date in the upper right corner of the first clean page. Then he stares at that for a while. He could write about Richard forgetting to bring his skateboard to his house before going home, but that would only make him more annoyed. He was supposed to bring it and then stash it in his backyard. But he forgot. Gavin sighs and writes:

Well, I'm back. Nothing new to write about. Here's my new problem. Turns out I only have to walk the dog 30 minutes when I get home. But Aunt Myrtle doesn't even let me get a snack. There she is at the door ready to shove that horrible little Carlotta in my arms. That must be some kind of child abuse.

He stops to think about this. He bets it *is* child abuse — making a kid starve. Making a kid go into his own money that he's been saving and saving for a new skateboard, just to replace some crazy dog toy. The problem is that he knows no one would really think it's abuse. No grownups, anyway. They would think it's just a way of making him learn a lesson. How come grownups never have to learn lessons? It's not fair.

He goes back to his journal.

Today I'm going to run quick to the pet store and buy Carlotta another toy because I got the real one stolen. By this big dog in the park and I wasn't supposed to even be in the park. I had snuck over there to ride my skateboard. But this big guy

A hand comes down on his journal and attempts to pull it right out from under his pencil.

"Didn't you hear the teacher? She said for me to collect the journals." It's that bossy Deja girl. "She said pencils down, journals *closed*."

"But I thought the journals were collected only once a week."

"Ms. Shelby-*Ortiz*," Deja begins, as if she really loves saying the *Ortiz* part, "collects them a couple of times so she can check our spelling and skipped words and stuff and see if we're doing better."

"But I wasn't finished," Gavin protests.

"So? Too bad, so sad..." she says in a singsongy voice. She does this little thing with her neck when she says "sad." Gavin wonders if she's mad about something, or just mean. He watches her add his journal to the stack in her hand. Then she gives him a smile that looks more like a sneer before walking away. He watches her go. What's he ever done to *her*?

At recess, Richard is ball monitor. It's almost as good as Gavin being ball monitor, because as soon as they're out on the schoolyard, Richard passes the basketball to Gavin, who dribbles it all the way to the court, doing a really good dribble job and hoping everyone has stopped to notice. Well, he knows they haven't, but he can dream. When he gets there, he tries to do a layup just like he sees on TV, but the ball doesn't even get up to the basket. It arcs away from the court, and he has to go chasing after it. He hopes no one saw that.

Darnell's new friend Harper stops it with his foot. He's definitely getting a reputation for being someone to stay away from, even though he's only been at Carver Elementary a little while, like Gavin. Kids have been saying that Harper repeated third grade. And for some reason, this makes him seem a little bit scary. Probably because he really should be in sixth grade, and that's not even elementary school. That's middle school — a whole different story.

Harper just stands there, tall and big and looking stupid, with his foot on the basketball. He gives Gavin a menacing smile, reaches down, grabs the ball, and begins to toss it from one giant palm to the other. Then he begins to dribble it in a circle. Suddenly he stops and brings the ball to his chest like he's going to shoot it at Gavin.

Gavin holds his hands up, hopeful. But Harper only pretends that he's going to let go of the ball. He throws his head back and laughs really loud. Gavin feels his face heat up. Several of the boys from Room Ten have made their way over, and they've formed a semicircle around Gavin to watch what's happening. Gavin feels put on the spot as Harper fakes another throw. Without thinking, Gavin puts up his hands to catch. Harper laughs again, and several of Gavin's classmates join in. A few girls have even ambled over to see what's going on.

"Want it?" Harper calls out, now that he has an audience. "Come on, get ready!"

Gavin lets his hands hang. Then he brings them up again. If Harper really does throw that basketball, he could get hit hard. And that's not going to feel so good.

Harper does a few fakes, to the delight of everyone. The laughter grows louder. Gavin's face grows warmer.

Harper is in the middle of launching a new fake when suddenly Darnell comes out of nowhere and knocks the ball out of Harper's hand. He passes it to Gavin, who's ready and catches it, surprising himself.

"Come on, Harper," Darnell says. "Quit fooling around. We've got dodgeball this week, and you're wasting time."

While Harper seems to be deciding what he'll do, Gavin clutches the ball, feeling out of breath. He tries to calm his breathing. Harper turns on his heel and gallops off to the dodgeball court. Kids who have gathered, hoping for a show, stand around a bit and then mosey off to their own areas.

"Why did Darnell have to spoil the fun?" Gavin hears a girl from his class named Casey ask this other girl named Ayanna.

"Yeah, that was fun," Ayanna agrees.

● ● ●

"I gotta go to the pet store," Gavin says to Richard as they burst through the front doors after dismissal. For Gavin, this is the "free-est" time of day. He loves the feeling of his back to the school as he takes the front steps two at a time. When school is over, he can do almost anything he wants — for a little while. He can walk down Marin and stop by his uncle Vestor's best friend's store for candy, or he can go home and get permission to ride his bike for thirty minutes. He even likes standing at his kitchen counter, putting blobs of grape jelly on wheat crackers to eat while he does his homework.

Now Richard has to spoil it with, "Don't you have to go straight home to walk that dog?"

Gavin rolls his eyes. "I have to get a new chew toy first. Otherwise my aunt's going to have a fit. And I'm going to have to hear her say I'm irresponsible and a whole bunch of other stuff, and she might even have my mother put me on punishment."

"I'll go with you," Richard says.

So instead of turning toward Ashby, they head to Marin and Pet Mart, the big store that claims it has everything a pet owner could want or need for their beloved four-legged member of the family. Gavin figures if any place will have a toy that looks exactly like Carlotta's Chew-Chew, it's Pet Mart.

But when they get there, they discover that there's a whole aisle of rubber and rawhide knickknacks and thingamabobs for dogs to chew on. How will they ever find the right one? "What about this?" Richard asks, holding up a big round thing with what looks like a thousand rubber tentacles.

"No," Gavin says, shaking his head. "Her Chew-Chew doesn't look like that."

"Her what?"

"My aunt Myrtle calls it a Chew-Chew. It's this white rawhide bone thing with chewed-on knotted ends."

Richard moves down to one end of the aisle so he can start checking everything in it. Gavin goes to the other end and begins to move slowly in Richard's direction. So many doggie toys. He never knew dogs had such an array of toys devoted just to them. His eyes stop on something that looks a lot like Carlotta's Chew-Chew hanging on a shelf hook by a loop of twine. He takes it down and examines it closely. No, it's got little brown speckles on it. It won't do. It wouldn't fool Aunt Myrtle for a second.

He looks over at Richard, who is twirling a rope ball on a braided, twisted string. What in the world . . . ? Richard's supposed to be helping him. He knows Gavin has a time limit. What is he doing? Then Gavin sees Richard pick up a bag of dog biscuits from a display at the end of the aisle, gaze at them, then sniff them. He looks like he wants to eat one.

"Richard!" Gavin hisses. "What are you doing?"

Richard looks over at him and grins. "These look good," he says.

"Are you crazy? Those are for dogs! Come on. You gotta help me!"

"Oh, yeah," Richard says. Slowly he begins walking back down the aisle toward Gavin, looking closely at the items on the shelves. "What about this?" He holds up a dark beige dog chew.

"Wrong color," Gavin says. He checks the big round clock on the store wall. Three ten. *Oh, no.* He imagines Aunt Myrtle checking the clock on the kitchen stove right then. He turns back to the shelves and keeps searching.

"What about this?"

Gavin sighs and looks at what Richard's holding up. He moves closer. Richard has a hard rawhide bone that looks a lot like the Chew-Chew. Same color, same size.

"Let me see that," he says.

Richard hands the bone over for Gavin to examine. It could definitely pass for Carlotta's Chew-Chew. "I think this is it," he says. "This one is new, but I bet I can dirty it up.

Make it look a lot like the real thing." Gavin looks at Richard with new respect. He knew there was a brain in there somewhere.

"Let's go to Mr. D.'s store for chips," Richard suggests as they pay and leave the store.

"I gotta get home, Richard," Gavin says, stuffing the Chew-Chew into his backpack.

"We'll go real quick."

"I don't know . . ."

"We'll be in and out, Gavin. I promise."

"We better," Gavin says. They turn toward Ashby.

● ● ●

Gavin spots Darnell, Gregory Johnson, and Harper as soon as he and Richard walk into Mr. D.'s store. A feeling of unease comes over him. Because of Harper, he really doesn't want to go near the group. But before Gavin can stop Richard, he calls out, "Hey, whatcha guys getting?" and makes his way over to his brother.

Darnell is looking at the display of chips. Gregory Johnson is scanning the shelves of candy right in front of the register. Harper has disappeared down one of the aisles.

"I don't know yet, so you mind?" With the back of his hand, Darnell gently moves Richard, who's blocking his view, out of the way of the chip display. Gavin looks up at the big security mirror that reflects everybody who can't be seen from the cash register, then glances at Mr. Delvecchio. He's busy ringing up a Big Chunk candy bar for Gregory. Gavin looks back at the mirror and sees Harper running his fingers over a rack of those cheap toys that break after you've played with them only a couple of times: water pistols and rubber balls attached to wooden paddles, small plastic cars. He settles on a spiky rubber-ball thing. He removes it from the rack and, instead of taking it up to the register, he slips it inside his jacket under his arm.

Gavin feels his eyes grow big. Real big. He can't look away. Mr. Delvecchio is putting Gregory Johnson's candy bar in a small bag. Gavin watches Harper come down the aisle with his hands in his jacket pockets, whistling. He goes straight up to the counter. Gavin knows why he's got his hands in his pockets. He knows why he's keeping his upper arms pressed to his sides. Because his left arm is keeping the toy from falling to the floor.

Gavin feels his heart pounding in

his chest. He stares at Harper, who's now whistling something that doesn't even sound like a real tune. "What's taking you guys so long?" Harper says to Gregory and Darnell. "I gotta go."

Gavin looks at Mr. Delvecchio again. He can see that Mr. D. doesn't know what Harper did. For some strange reason, Gavin feels guilty. It's as if he has taken the toy himself. Mr. Delvecchio and his uncle are friends. Harper might as well have stolen from Uncle Vestor.

"Hey, whatcha know good?" Mr. D. says suddenly, turning to Gavin. "What's your uncle up to?" The older boys walk out the door. Mr. Delvecchio rings up Richard's bag of chips and drops the change in his hand.

"He's at some kind of conference for barbershop people," Gavin answers quietly.

"Tell him I'm waiting to challenge him at dominoes. It's been a while."

"Yes, sir," Gavin says. He nudges Richard in the side and nods quickly toward the door. Richard frowns, puzzled.

As soon as they get outside, Gavin points at Harper with his hands still in his pockets, sauntering down Fulton with the older boys a half block ahead. "That guy's a thief!" he whispers.

"What?" Richard follows his pointing finger. "Who's a thief? Not my brother. He's never stolen anything in his life."

"No, not your brother — and not Gregory Johnson, either." Gavin squints. "I'm talking about Harper. I saw him in that mirror thing that's supposed to make it so a store person can see who's stealing stuff. I saw him put a toy — you know, one of those balls covered with those spiky things — in his jacket."

"In his jacket?"

"Didn't you see how he was walking with his arms all pressed against his body?"

"Yeah," Richard says slowly, like he's not really sure. He stares at Harper now. "He still has his hands in his pockets."

"I betcha he steals all the time," Gavin says.

"He probably has a whole room full of stolen stuff. They go to the store every day after school," Richard says, nodding slowly like he's a detective.

"I should tell Mr. D. to watch him more closely. I can tell him I heard Harper steals, and that he should be really careful when Harper comes in his store," Gavin says.

"But then what if Mr. D. tells Harper that you're the one who told on him?" Richard asks. "Harper's a big guy."

"I know he's a big guy," Gavin says, annoyed. "You don't need to tell me that."

So what should he do? Gavin thinks about this all the way home. He gives a wave to Richard when he turns toward his house on Fulton and Gavin turns toward his house on Willow. Quietly, he makes his way to his backyard, almost tiptoeing as he passes under the kitchen window. He unzips his backpack and takes out the new chew toy. Just then he hears the kitchen door open.

"And where have you been, mister?" Aunt Myrtle is standing on the top step with her hands on her hips.

Before he turns around to answer, he slips the new chew toy into his jacket.

"Oh, uh, I had something to do after school." It's a lame excuse, but before Aunt Myrtle can think about it too carefully, he adds, "But I came as fast as I could after that."

Aunt Myrtle looks at him hard. She sighs. "Well, you're here now. Stay right there while I get Carlotta." Before she opens the door, she calls over her shoulder, "And where on earth is Carlotta's Chew-Chew?"

Gavin thinks fast. "Uh, I think it's in the bushes." He's proud that he's managed not to tell a big lie. After all, he was going to rub it in the dirt by the bushes and leave it there.

"What's it doing in the bushes?" Aunt Myrtle says almost to herself as she heads back into the house.

Gavin stoops down to roll the chew toy around in the dirt. When he's finished, he holds it up. It kind of looks like the old Chew-Chew.

Aunt Myrtle is back on the porch with Carlotta in her arms. "I certainly wish you'd told me that thing was in the bushes. She's been whimpering for it all day."

Gavin looks at Carlotta. Immediately she starts yap-yapping as if she's got some fussing to do at Gavin too. He sighs. How many more days of this does he have to endure? Two. Just two — after today. He doesn't know if he'll survive.

"Let me have the thing," Aunt Myrtle says.

Gavin hands it over and watches Aunt Myrtle closely to see if she notices anything. She takes it in her hand and, before giving it to Carlotta, looks at it carefully. She turns it this way and that. Gavin can't tell what she's thinking. She nuzzles Carlotta's nose with it. Carlotta turns her head, drawing back a little. "Well, that's a first," Aunt Myrtle says, putting Carlotta down and handing the leash and a plastic bag to Gavin. "I suppose a dog can outgrow a toy too." She shakes her head as she goes back into the house.

Gavin realizes he's been holding his breath and lets it out with a whoosh.

Halfway down the block, dear Carlotta rewards Gavin with a wonderful prize for all his efforts, in the grass right next to his neighbor Mrs. Marvin's rosebush. Well, at least he's got that handy plastic bag, and at least tomorrow is trash day. He only has to lift up Mrs. Marvin's trash can lid and slip the "prize" in there. He doesn't have to walk all over the place with that . . . *thing* in his hand.

Ugh! Even though he used the plastic bag, somehow his hand still feels *dirty*. He can't wait to get home and wash his hands ten times.

Seven
Harper's Not Happy

All the way to school the next day, Gavin repeats to himself, "Just today and tomorrow. Just today and tomorrow, and then I'm free." *He can do it. He will survive.* There *is* a light at the end of the tunnel. He still has a smile on his face when he makes his way across the yard to where Room Ten lines up. It will be so good to get back to his regular after-school routine.

He slips in line in front of that really snooty girl, Antonia. She turns around and gives him a look that makes him wonder if he forgot to wash his face or something. Richard, who is a bit late getting there, moves in behind Antonia. The two fifth grade classes are already lined up in perfect formation. Except for Harper. He keeps turning around to look at . . . *Gavin*. Uh-oh. What could *that* be about? Gavin turns around, thinking perhaps Harper's mean look is aimed at someone behind him. But, no, there are mostly girls behind him. Harper's scary eyes are focused only on Gavin. That snarly look is aimed at *him*. He swallows hard. What's he done? Why's Harper giving him that look? Unless —

Gavin whips around and looks at Richard. "Richard," he hisses.

"Whoa," that Antonia girl says. "Say it, don't spray it!" She wipes her face in disgust.

Gavin looks around to see who might have heard her. He feels his face grow warm.

"You're gonna get us in trouble," Antonia continues. "We're not supposed to be talking."

Ms. Shelby-Ortiz is crossing the yard toward the line. Suddenly everyone is standing ramrod straight, staring at the back of the head of the person in front of them, lips pressed together. Ms. Shelby-Ortiz looks up and down the line and gives a little nod. This week's line leader, Carlos, takes the class to Room Ten.

● ● ●

"What did you want?" Richard asks as they put their lunches and backpacks in their cubbies.

"How come Harper was giving me mean looks?"

"I don't know," says Richard, but his eyes look shifty.

"Did you tell Harper what I said about him?"

"What was that?" Richard asks.

"That I saw him steal that toy at Mr. Delvecchio's store."

Richard doesn't answer right away. Then he says, "I don't know. Maybe I told my brother."

"Why would you do that? You knew he'd tell Harper. Now I think Harper's mad at me."

"Well — " Richards starts, but he's cut off by Ms. Shelby-Ortiz.

"I'm waiting for everyone to be in their seats and ready to work." She looks directly at Gavin and Richard. They put their conversation on hold and move to their desks.

● ● ●

As soon as they're on the yard for morning recess, Gavin corners Richard before he can run off to the basketball court. He looks around for Harper but doesn't see him. "You have to tell me now," Gavin says. "What do you think Harper knows?"

"I don't know," Richard says, looking past Gavin.

"What's that supposed to mean?"

"I told Darnell, and I guess he could have told Harper."

"Thanks. A lot."

"But maybe he didn't tell him."

"Yeah, right." Gavin sighs. Now what is he going to do? He looks around again for Harper. "Wonder where he's at?"

Richard offers, "He's benched today and tomorrow. For not doing his homework."

Gavin looks over toward the "benched kids" area that's reserved for students who have misbehaved: talking back to the teacher, fighting instead of using their words, not doing their homework. Sure enough, there's Harper, looking glum, with his chin resting on his palm, frowning. *He probably feels that he shouldn't have to do any homework,* Gavin thinks from his safe distance near the basketball court.

"Good," Gavin says. "Maybe he'll forget all about what your brother told him by the time Monday comes."

"What's that?" Richard says.

"That I said I saw him stealing." Richard could act so stupid at times.

"That's not exactly what I said, actually," Richard

corrects him. "I kind of told Darnell that you said Harper was a *thief.*"

● ● ●

Now Gavin has to look over his shoulder all the way home.

"What's the problem?" Richard asks as he walks beside him. "Why do you keep looking back?"

"I'm lookin' to see where Harper is."

"Why?"

"'Cause he's probably after me."

"You're scared?"

"What do you think? And you'd be too if someone told Harper you called him a thief."

Richard raises his eyebrows as if he's thinking about the situation for the first time. "Okay, okay. We just need to go another way. Like maybe down that street where the Food Barn is, then cut across to Ashby, then down to Maynard. We can take that to your street, but we'll be coming up to it from the other end. Simple."

Not so simple, Gavin thinks as he allows Richard to lead the way. All the way down Post, Gavin feels okay, but as soon as they reach Ashby, a busier street, he starts looking over his shoulder again, expecting to see that Harper has just magically appeared behind him. Luckily, every time he looks back, he sees that the sidewalk is empty.

Once they reach the corner, Gavin puts a hand on Richard's shoulder. "Wait." He looks both ways to see if the coast is clear. Amazingly, there's no sign of Harper — nor Darnell and Gregory Johnson. They cross the street at the light at Maynard, and Gavin is a little relieved. Halfway down the block, Richard turns off on Fulton. "See ya," he calls over his shoulder. Gavin feels a tiny bit abandoned as he continues on to his street.

○ ○ ○

"Finally," Aunt Myrtle huffs, opening the door just as he's coming up the walkway. Of course, Carlotta is in her arms, wiggling and making that high-pitched whine that evil little dogs make all the time. She's actually scrambling to get out of Aunt Myrtle's arms. Almost, he realizes, as if she's . . . looking forward to him and their walk. For a moment Gavin almost feels . . . special. *Naw,* he thinks. All dogs like to get out of the house. All dogs like to *go.*

Aunt Myrtle hands him the plastic bag and the leash, which is already attached to Carlotta's collar. She sets Carlotta down. The dog practically pulls Gavin down the steps. He's barely able to toss his backpack onto the porch as she drags him away. Aunt Myrtle throws Carlotta a kiss. "Goodbye, precious. Have a good time."

Gavin decides to go by the park. Other folks walk their dogs there, so why not him? Aunt Myrtle didn't give him a chance to grab his board, which Richard had finally returned after dinner the previous night, but he can still go and watch the skaters. No one ever said he had to walk blocks and blocks all around the neighborhood with Carlotta. Why not just walk around the skate park? Gavin turns in that direction. He wonders if he was worried about Harper for nothing. Harper is probably at Homework Club. That's where all the benched kids have to go after school. So the coast was probably clear all along. He laughs to himself, imagining big, hulky Harper chewing on his pencil trying to figure out two times five.

He walks once around the skate park and then branches out a little farther. He doesn't see Richard, Darnell, or Gregory Johnson. Carlotta seems happy. She bounces along beside him like she's been freed from prison. On the third time around the skate park, she stops to take care of her business. Gavin's ready with the plastic bag. He's gotten kind of used to it. The trick is to take care of the task quickly, before he can think about it too much. He's just deposited the plastic bag in the big trash can near the basketball courts and is wondering where Richard is when someone taps him on the shoulder.

"I see you still got that ugly little dog."

It's *not* Richard's voice. It's *Harper's*. When Gavin turns around, he's staring up into his angry face. He doesn't know what to say. His mouth doesn't seem to want to open. He looks down at Carlotta, at the stupid pink bows in the tufts of hair by each ear — at the little rhinestone collar. He keeps his mouth shut.

"Anyway, I heard you called me a thief." Harper gives Gavin's shoulder a poke. A hard poke. He glares down at him.

Gavin bites his lip but still says nothing. Maybe Harper will be satisfied with just giving him a sharp poke on the shoulder and will go away.

"What do you have to say about that?"

Gavin doesn't have anything to say.

"I don't hear you," Harper says, with another poke to Gavin's shoulder. Now Gavin is pretty sure Harper is not going to be satisfied with two hard pokes.

"I — saw you steal that toy," Gavin says.

"What? You saw *what*?"

It feels like a challenge. Gavin gathers his courage and repeats, "I saw you steal that toy and put it in your jacket."

"You're a liar," Harper says, raising his voice.

Gavin's mouth drops open in fear and surprise. How can Harper call him a liar when he *knows* good and well what he did? But then, behind Harper, he sees that tall guy from the day before, the one with the big shaggy dog, coming toward them. Suddenly the tall guy is putting his hand on Harper's head like a hat.

Harper frowns, and then looks puzzled.

"What's the problem here?" the guy asks.

Harper wrenches around angrily and opens his mouth to protest. But he has to look up to meet the guy's eyes, and just that fact makes him get quiet real fast.

"I'm not liking what I'm seeing," the guy continues. "I might be seeing a big bully here, and I'm not liking it."

Harper glares at Gavin, but keeps his mouth shut.

"Look here," the big guy says to Gavin while staring down at Harper. "I'm here every day. You let me know if you have any more trouble out of this kid — and tell me where he lives. I'll go have a little talk with his parents."

Harper's eyes get big at that.

"Why don't you just go play in the sandbox or something and leave this little guy alone?"

Harper gives Gavin one more warning look, but he doesn't dare say anything. Slowly he saunters off as if he's not one bit scared, but Gavin bets he is.

Gavin doesn't get it. The tall guy hadn't been very honest or fair to Gavin just two days before. Why was he being so nice now? What was going on? Whatever the reason, Gavin is glad to be spared from Harper's anger, even though he doesn't know what Harper will do the next day. He hopes he'll keep that big guy in mind.

"Thanks," Gavin says as he starts to move away with Carlotta.

"Wait a sec," the guy says. He reaches into his jacket pocket and pulls out Carlotta's Chew-Chew. "This is yours. I don't know why I kept it. Sorry." Now he gives Gavin a big smile of apology. Gavin takes the toy out of his hand, but he's still confused — and a little bit annoyed that he spent part of his savings on that new chew toy. Oh, well. He supposes Carlotta can't have too many Chew-Chews.

"Thank you." It's all he can think to say.

Eight
Where Did Carlotta Go?

Last day! Last day! The words pop into Gavin's head as soon as his eyes open. He listens to the morning sounds downstairs. Carlotta's doing her usual yapping from behind the child's gate that's keeping her on the back porch. Aunt Myrtle is shuffling down the stairs to the kitchen. Gavin thinks that's a wonderful sound, because it reminds him that Uncle Vestor returns tomorrow and it's going to be bye-bye, Carlotta. Bye-bye, Aunt Myrtle. And bye-bye, picking-up-dog-poop.

Gavin bounds down the stairs, sniffing the air for the scent of French toast. His mother always fixes French toast on Fridays, as a sort of celebration of the coming weekend. Sure enough, his mom is just putting a stack of French toast on the table. His father is behind his newspaper, and Aunt Myrtle is sitting across from him, sipping her tea. Danielle is sitting in her usual seat, sneaking looks at her phone on her lap. Should he tell on her? Nah, he feels too good about it being Friday and his last day of having to deal with Carlotta.

"Good morning," Gavin says as he takes his seat, trying not to sound too happy.

"Good morning, sweetie," his mom replies, dishing two pieces of French toast onto his plate.

"Morning," his father says from behind his paper.

Danielle rolls her eyes. He's not surprised.

Aunt Myrtle blows on her tea. "Good morning, Gavin. I think this must be payday. As soon as you walk Carlotta this afternoon, that is."

Gavin looks over at the dog. *Last day, horrible little doggie,* he thinks. He takes a big bite of French toast.

● ● ●

On the way to school, Richard notices his good mood. "You've been whistling since we turned the corner. How come?"

"This is my last day walking Carlotta. And it's Friday. There's no homework on Fridays. I get to stay up an extra hour on Fridays. We have spelling tests on Fridays, and I always get a hundred percent. Um . . ."

"Okay, okay," Richard says. "I get it. When do you get paid?"

"After I walk Carlotta one last time."

"Good. Even *I* can't wait."

"There *is* one little thing I might be worried about today, though."

"What?"

"I hope Harper is still benched."

● ● ●

When Ms. Shelby-Ortiz leads the class out for recess, Gavin is almost afraid to look over at the benched kids. He takes a quick peek. There's Harper, sitting facing the yard, all sprawled out, the backs of his elbows resting on the table behind him. Gavin can't see his face, but imagines his lip curled in anger. He looks away quickly, afraid that Harper might catch him staring.

"He's benched," Richard whispers behind him. "Lighten up."

Lunchtime presents more opportunities to run into Harper. Room Ten's lunch table is three tables behind the one assigned to Harper's class. Gavin sits down and sets his lunch (a sandwich, chips, and an apple) before him, but doesn't feel hungry.

"Can I have those chips?" Richard asks.

Gavin doesn't answer. He's busy looking at Harper's mean face as he sits hunched at his table eating chocolate chip cookies. He's even eating the cookies in a hostile way, breaking off little chunks, popping them into his mouth, and chomping on them with a sneer. At one point he looks up and glares at Gavin. Gavin looks down quickly and busies himself with his own lunch.

● ● ●

"I'm telling you, he gave me a real dirty look," Gavin says to Richard on their way to the handball court.

"So what?" Richard says. "He's benched. He can't do anything to you even if he wanted to."

Gavin sneaks a quick peek over at the benched kids. Harper sits in the middle of the group, his chin on his hand and his elbow on his knee, still with the mean look on his face. *Saved by the bench*, Gavin thinks.

He almost manages to get through the day without seeing Harper again. But then, after P.E., Ms. Shelby-Ortiz has the boys and girls line up at the boys' and girls' restrooms, as usual. She lets three boys and three girls go in at a time. As soon as Gavin enters with Carlos and Jose, he runs into Harper. His hall pass is on the sink in front of him. He is wetting bits of balled paper towel and then throwing them up at the ceiling, where they stick. He's so busy breaking a school rule that he doesn't even notice Gavin.

Gavin immediately makes a U-turn and exits the restroom, his heart beating fast, even though he really has to go. What a close call.

"Ms. Shelby-Ortiz," he says as soon as they get back to class and he's seated. He hadn't even raised his hand and waited to be recognized. "May I go to the bathroom?"

"What?" she answers. "Didn't you just go to the restroom?" There must be something about the panic in his face that makes her say, "Oh, all right, get going."

He jumps up and practically runs out of the classroom.

● ● ●

When the dismissal bell rings, Gavin feels as if he's been dodging danger all day long.

"I have to walk Carlotta, but since there's no homework, let's meet at the skate park later. I'm sure I can get permission," Gavin says to Richard as they hurry down Marin on their new route from school. They part at Fulton.

Gavin is anxious to get the last walk with Carlotta over and done with. Maybe, since it's his last time walking her, Aunt Myrtle will let him have his snack first.

He decides he will propose this to her, but when Aunt Myrtle opens the door, she seems frantic. She steps out onto the porch and looks up and down the street. "Have you seen Carlotta?"

"No," Gavin says slowly. He looks past Aunt Myrtle down the hall, expecting to hear Carlotta's toenails clicking on the floor. But Carlotta is nowhere to be seen. Aunt Myrtle steps around Gavin and ventures down the porch steps. She reaches the sidewalk and walks a few feet in one direction and then the other, shielding her eyes as she peers up and down the street. "I just put her out in the yard for a bit, and when I came out to get her"—Aunt Myrtle pats her chest as if overcome—"she was gone! There's a spot where she must have dug herself out under the fence. I don't even know why she would do this. I don't know . . ." Aunt Myrtle's voice trails off. But then she adds, "And she doesn't have her collar on! I'd taken it off because it was causing a little irritation. I couldn't find her other one . . ." Her voice trails off again, and she turns and climbs the steps to go back into the house. Gavin follows, not knowing what to think. Does this mean he can go into the kitchen and make his special snack?

Then his mother comes down the staircase. "Sweetie,

did you see Carlotta? Maybe down the street somewhere while you were walking home?"

"No, I haven't seen her anywhere." He looks over at Aunt Myrtle, who has collapsed into a chair in the living room and is fanning herself with a folded paper.

"Can you go out and look around a bit for her?"

Gavin thinks longingly of his snack. It looks like he won't be heading for the kitchen to make it after all. Again.

"Don't go past Marin or the park," his mother adds, stepping out onto the porch to look up and down the street herself.

As soon as he starts up the block, Gavin begins to feel funny. Carlotta is out there somewhere, and a tiny pinprick of worry tickles him. He walks toward Marin, listening for sounds of distant barking. Not deep barking, but Carlotta's particular little yap-yap bark. He hears nothing. The empty streets make it seem as if she's simply disappeared. *Maybe she's been dognapped,* he thinks as he hurries down the street. Or maybe Richard's seen Carlotta.

When he reaches the skate park, Richard is busy practicing

his flat-ground Ollie on the cinderblock ledge. Gavin stands at the chainlink fence and watches him approach the block and then chicken out at the last minute. He tries again, and this time he gets the front of the board up, but then lets it plop back down. Luckily, no one's waiting to use the ledge.

"Richard!" Gavin calls before he can make his next attempt.

Richard whips around, looking surprised. "I thought you couldn't come until after you walked that dog." He moves to the fence with his skateboard in his hand, looking puzzled. "Where's your skateboard?"

"Have you seen Carlotta?" Gavin asks, already having a pretty good idea of what Richard's going to say.

"No, why?"

"She's missing."

"Missing?"

"My aunt put her in the backyard, and she dug a hole under the fence and got out."

"Why'd she do that?" Richard asks.

"How am I supposed to know? It's a dog thing. Dogs like

to dig holes and they like to get out of their yards." Gavin shrugs.

Richard nods slowly, as if that makes sense to him. "Want me to help you look?"

"Yeah," Gavin says. "But my mom doesn't want me to go past Marin."

"Well, what if she went all the way to that big street with the tire shop, or maybe over to the pet store where we got that toy?"

"I don't know," Gavin says. "My mom'll probably get my father to look around those places when he gets home from work."

Together, they begin to call out Carlotta's name as they start toward Marin. "Carlotta! Carlotta!" People stop what they're doing for a moment to take in the fact that someone, or someone's pet, has gotten lost. The mailman waves, and the guy from S&L Nursery looks up from watering a row of ficus trees. Two girls stop jumping double dutch on the walkway in front of a house next to the nursery. One of them walks over to Richard and Gavin.

"Who's Carlotta?" she asks. Gavin recognizes her from one of the other third grades at Carver Elementary. Her friend comes over too.

"Yeah, who's Carlotta?" her friend repeats.

"My aunt's dog got out of our yard and ran away," Gavin explains. "Have you seen a stray dog?"

"What's she look like?" the taller girl asks, biting her thumbnail.

Gavin doesn't have much hope she'll be helpful. But before he can answer, Richard pipes up with, "She's one of those funny-looking kind of dogs. Kind of small. Ugly-looking fur."

Gavin surprises himself. He's growing annoyed by this description of Carlotta. For some reason, he feels the need to stick up for her. "She's not all that funny-looking," he interrupts. "You guys know what a Pomeranian looks like?"

"A what-a-ranian?" the shorter girl asks. She laughs at her own joke. Then her friend joins in.

Gavin was right. He knew they wouldn't be helpful. He's ready to move on. "Never mind. Come on, let's go," he says to Richard.

They cover the rest of Marin as far as the park, then go down Ashby toward Richard's house, on Fulton, where they part. Then it's back home. Gavin's mother meets him at the door with questions before he can even step inside.

Apparently, she's sent Danielle out to search for Carlotta as well. Aunt Myrtle is nowhere to be seen.

"I told Aunt Myrtle to go upstairs and lie down," his mom explains. "Your dad is out in his car looking too."

"Can I make a snack?" Gavin asks. Now he's really hungry.

"Yeah, yeah. Go get your snack," his mother says as if her mind is on something else.

Gavin hurries into the kitchen before his mother can change her mind. He takes the jar of grape jelly out of the refrigerator, unscrews the lid, and inhales deeply. *Ahh, what an awesome smell,* he thinks. He gets a plate out of the cabinet, takes down the box of wheat crackers, gets a knife, and goes to work. On the plate are five crackers spread with purple jelly.

Before he carries his snack to the kitchen, he pops one in his mouth. *Delicious,* he thinks. He pops another one in his mouth. At that moment, there is nothing tastier in the world.

● ● ●

Dinner is quiet. Aunt Myrtle has come down from the guest room, but she says very little, and the worried crease never leaves her brow. She's given Gavin's dad the picture of Carlotta that she usually keeps in a frame on the nightstand by her bed. Gavin's dad plans to make flyers with the picture on them, to post all over the neighborhood. But for now, Aunt Myrtle just sits there, staring at her green beans, lamb chops, and mashed potatoes.

"Aunt Myrtle, why don't you try to eat a little something?" Gavin's mom suggests.

"I can't eat," Aunt Myrtle says. "I don't have an appetite. Your uncle Vestor's going to be sick with worry. Carlotta's his dog too." She sighs and shakes her head.

Gavin wonders if Uncle Vestor knows already, or if he'll find out when he returns in the morning.

"I'm just going to go back upstairs and lie down." Aunt Myrtle pushes back her chair. Everyone is silent as they watch her shuffle off.

"We've got to find Carlotta," Gavin's mother says once Aunt Myrtle is out of earshot. "I don't know what's going to happen if we don't find that dog."

"I'll make the flyers tonight, then we'll post them in as many places as we can in the morning," his dad says.

○ ○ ○

On Saturday morning, Aunt Myrtle mopes about while the rest of them eat a quick breakfast. As soon as they've finished, Gavin's dad hands stacks of the flyers to Danielle and Gavin to take to the shops on Marin and Ashby. He's got the big staple gun in his hand. He'll be posting flyers on the telephone poles all around the neighborhood.

The strange thing is that Gavin didn't sleep well the night before. He kept waking up, *worried about Carlotta.* What if the silly dog thought she could beat up that big dog they encountered the first day he walked her? What if she got in that dog's yard, thinking she could take him on? Do dogs do those kinds of things? What if she was hungry — or thirsty? He worried that he hadn't yet exchanged the real Chew-Chew for the fake one. What if she never got to be reunited with the toy that she loved so much?

His shoulders slump. So much to worry about.

"You take Marin," Danielle orders. "I'll take Ashby."

"Why do I have to take Marin?" Gavin asks, not knowing why he's asking that. He doesn't really trust his sister. Maybe she has some kind of trick planned.

"Fine, Bozo. I'll take Marin, and you can take Ashby."
Danielle shrugs. "You're such a dork."

● ● ●

Gavin goes to Babe's Barbecue first. There's no one inside. Mr. Olive, who is Babe (he must have thought it was a catchy name), is hosing down his front walkway.

"Mr. Olive, have you seen this dog?"

Mr. Olive looks at the flyer in Gavin's hand. He studies it. "Can't say that I have," he answers.

"Can you put this poster in your store window?"

"Sure. Go put it on the counter."

Gavin goes to Global Tire and Brakes, Perfect Beauty Hair Salon and Nail Emporium, and the Re-Sell Shop. Everyone at the stores on Ashby is sympathetic. They must see the worry in his eyes. They look at the poster, shake their heads, and then promise to put up the flyer in their windows. Gavin is hot and thirsty by the time he finishes with Ashby. He decides to go by Richard's house on his way home. See what he's up to. Maybe get something to drink.

Nine
Is That Carlotta?

Richard is sitting on his front porch tossing a tennis ball up in the air. Darnell is just leaving on his bike. He gives Gavin a quick "Hi," and then he's off.

"What's up?" Richard asks. "What are those for?" He points to the stack of flyers in Gavin's hand.

"Carlotta is still lost. We're posting these around the neighborhood. Want to help?"

"Okay," Richard says. "But I have to get permission."

"Can I have something to drink? I'm thirsty."

"Yeah, sure."

Gavin's never been in Richard's house before. He's surprised to see how messy it is. Maybe it's because there are a lot of boys in Richard's family. There's Richard; Darnell, in fifth grade; Jamal, in seventh; and Roland, in the ninth grade. Dishes are piled in the sink. There are soccer jerseys draped over the kitchen chairs. A basketball sits in the corner. Cereal boxes are left out in the middle of the table. Gavin thinks of the things his mother would say if she walked into their kitchen and it looked like that. He can just hear the shock in her voice, all the fussing she'd do. Richard finds a clean glass and fills it with water. Gavin gulps it down gratefully while Richard goes off to ask for permission to help with the flyers.

Once they're back outside on the porch, Richard says, "Wait here. I'm going to get my scooter from out back."

"But I don't have my scooter," Gavin says.

"I'll get my skateboard. You can use that."

Gavin sits down on the top step to wait. He looks up the street in one direction and then the other. Way down at the end of the block, on the other side of the street, he sees two girls from his class. The mean girl, Deja, and that other girl. He forgets her name. They're each walking a dog. It's funny, but one of the dogs looks a little bit like Carlotta. It has almost the same color fur — but maybe darker, he thinks. Deja is walking the other dog. It has a small, thin body and long legs, and a pointy face. He watches for a bit and then turns his attention to the guy across the street washing his car. It's a black car with shiny pipes coming out of the back and some spokey-looking hubcaps. Gavin decides he's going to get a car like that when he gets to be that guy's age. He looks up the street again. The girls with the dog that looks like Carlotta have gotten closer.

Gavin stands up and shields his eyes. Wait a minute! As Deja and her friend approach, he sees one of the little dogs pull at the leash just like Carlotta used to do. Then the dog stops to sniff the grass. The nicer girl — Nikki, he now remembers — has to tug her along, the same way he used to have to do with Carlotta. Slowly it begins to dawn on Gavin. That little dog *is* Carlotta! What are *they* doing with her? At that moment Richard comes around the side of the house on his scooter with his skateboard under his arm.

"That's Carlotta!" Gavin exclaims to him.

"What?" Richard asks. He looks confused.

"Those girls have Aunt Myrtle's dog! That's Carlotta!" He points down the block at Deja and Nikki.

"How come they've got your aunt's dog?" Richard asks.

"I don't know," Gavin says. He runs to the curb, looks both ways, then crosses the street to meet the girls.

Carlotta seems just as happy prancing along or stopping in her tracks to sniff at the grass as she was when Gavin walked her. He can't believe it. He hurries to them, and the bossy one, Deja, frowns in recognition. What did he ever do to *her?* She takes the leash out of Nikki's hand and pulls Carlotta to her as Gavin approaches.

"Where'd you get that dog?" he says when he's close enough to be heard.

"Why?" Deja asks.

"Because that's not your dog!" He points at Carlotta.

"How do you know?" the nicer girl asks in a quiet voice.

"That's my aunt's dog! She got out of our yard yesterday, and we've been looking all over for her." He looks down at Carlotta, who still seems perfectly pleased to be in the possession of people who are complete strangers. He finds himself annoyed. It's as if she's some kind of traitor. The other dog is trying to pull Deja toward a candy wrapper on the grass.

"How do we know that's true?" Deja asks.

Richard has crossed the street and joined the group. Now he adds, "That *is* his aunt's dog. He's been walking that dog after school every day this week."

"Well, then how come she's acting like you're a stranger?" Deja asks.

Gavin looks down at Carlotta. "Carlotta," he says. The dog pays him no mind. She's back to sniffing at the grass. "Carlotta," he says again.

"See?" Deja says. "She doesn't even know you."

"Okay, then, where did you get this dog?" Gavin challenges her.

Before Deja can open her mouth, the other girl says, "We happened to save this dog's life. She was almost going to get hit by a car, and we stopped her before she crossed in front of it. Anyway, my parents said that she's a stray, just like Deja's dog, Ms. Precious Penelope. She didn't even have a collar, and they said I could keep her if no one claimed her, and we're going to take her to the vet for her shots and stuff."

"Nikki, you don't have to tell him all that."

It's just then that Gavin realizes he's left proof that the dog is his aunt's on Richard's porch. Again, he looks both ways down the empty street and then dashes across. He gathers the flyers and hurries back to the group.

"Look at this," he says, holding up a flyer close to Deja's nose. She bats at it and backs away. But she reads it. And her friend Nikki reads it too.

HAVE YOU SEEN THIS DOG?

Her name is Carlotta and she is the beloved companion of Mrs. Myrtle Roberts.
She has orange-brown fur and was not wearing her collar when she ran off
on Friday afternoon.
She's been missing for the last 24 hours.
If you see her or know where she is,
please contact Myrtle Roberts at 555-3423.

555-3423 555-3423 555-3423 555-3423 555-3423 555-3423 555-3423 555-3423 555-3423 555-3423 555-3423 555-3423 555-3423 555-3423 555-3423 555-3423 555-3423 555-34

Under the paragraph is the picture of Carlotta. She has a jumbo pink bow in her hair. Nikki and Deja stare at it. They look down at Carlotta, still doing her sniffing routine, then back at the flyer.

"Well, I want my leash and collar back," Nikki says sadly. "I knew it was too good to be true," she adds, more to herself than anyone else.

"I'll give them back on Monday at school," Gavin says, scooping Carlotta up in his arms.

○ ○ ○

Gavin feels like a real hero when he climbs the steps of his porch with Carlotta squirming in his arms. Richard is right behind him, probably not wanting to miss the hero's welcome his friend is about to receive. Before Richard can get the front door for Gavin, Uncle Vestor opens it. When he sees them, his eyes grow big and his lips part, but no sound comes out. Then he yells, "Myrtle, get in here!" His voice brings Gavin's dad (back from posting flyers) and Gavin's mom running too. They stand there together staring at Carlotta in stunned silence for a moment. It's as if they can't believe their eyes.

"Where did you find her?" his mom finally asks while Aunt Myrtle takes the dog out of his arms and gives her a

hug. Danielle walks in the door just then with a few leftover flyers in her hand. Even *her* mouth drops open at the sight of Carlotta.

"These two girls on Richard's street had her. They said they saved her from getting hit by a car. And that they didn't know she belonged to anyone, because she didn't have a collar."

"It's a miracle," Aunt Myrtle says. "A miracle." She takes Carlotta into the living room and sits down on the sofa.

Uncle Vestor walks over to Gavin and pats him on the back. His father stands there beaming. His mom smiles at him as well. Even Danielle is smiling at him. Now *that's* a real miracle.

"Well, Gavin, I think we need to do some settling up?" Uncle Vestor says.

Gavin frowns, not sure what that means, exactly. Uncle Vestor takes out his wallet and extracts two tens. "Here's what I owe you for walking Carlotta." He hands over one of the tens. "And this is what I owe you for finding Carlotta." He places the other ten in Gavin's hand. Gavin stares at the richness in his possession and whispers, "Thank you."

"Wow," Richard says appreciatively.

But before Gavin can savor his wealth, Danielle marches

over and plucks one of the tens out of his hand. "Thanks. This belongs to *me*," she says, and struts off to her room.

Gavin doesn't even mind. He is now finally *free* of his debt to his sister, Miss Danielle, Miss Know-It-All, Miss Just-Made-Teenager-Status. Oh, how good it feels. Plus he's got his own ten. This has been a great Saturday morning.

○ ○ ○

Later, as he and Richard are gliding on their skateboard and scooter to Miller's Park—after all the good-byes have been said to Aunt Myrtle and Uncle Vestor and, of course, dear Carlotta, and the real Chew-Chew has been handed over (Aunt Myrtle didn't even notice the difference)—Gavin feels a strange little twinge. An odd feeling that he just might, maybe, perhaps...No, it couldn't be. And yet, somehow, he thinks he possibly could—*miss* Carlotta. *And that would make three miracles in one day*, Gavin thinks, and smiles to himself. Then he pumps his foot against the concrete and sails past Richard toward the park.

Don't miss the next installment of
··THE CARVER CHRONICLES··

··THE CARVER CHRONICLES··

SKATEBOARD PARTY

BY KAREN ENGLISH
ILLUSTRATED BY Laura Freeman

Richard can't wait to show off his flat-ground Ollies at a friend's birthday party at the skate park, but a note home from his teacher threatens to ruin his plans. He really meant to finish his assignment on howler monkeys, but he just got . . . distracted. If only he could focus on his schoolwork, he wouldn't get into this kind of trouble! Can Richard manage to put off getting the note signed (and facing the consequences) until after the party, or will the deception make things even worse?